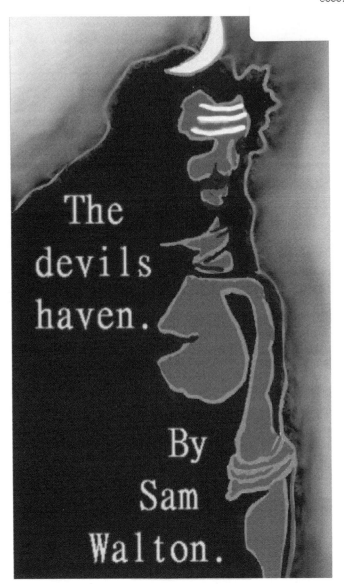

The
devils
haven.

By
Sam
Walton.

The devils
haven.

About the author.

Sam Walton is an up-and-coming author and artist, from a hard-working class background, in the East Midlands of England.

Sam first began writing as a form of therapy, to help him live with Schizophrenia and other Mental health conditions. Along with meditation and yoga, Sam's storytelling and art, allow his phenomenal imagination to find freedom on paper and joy to life.

Dedication.

I dedicate this book to my darling wife Sally, through whom, all things are possible.

The Rudra chronicles.

Book one.

San Diablo, the devils haven.

By Sam Walton.

Prologue.

The devil's haven is a story hinged around a top-secret prison in the middle of the scorching desert, far away from prying eyes. Our thrilling story is told through the words of a former inmate come yogic monk, the notorious Pappa Smurf. Our infamous narrator begins his action-packed story in a most unusual place by a most unusual person.

A tall, slender, but mean looking woman in her late twenties, walked through the old wooden doorway, into the back-office interview room, at the Daily Illumine press New York branch. She walked straight in, without knocking or announcing her presence to her invited guest.

The monk growled and raised an eyebrow in indignation, at the level of disrespect shown to him.

The tall Asian American woman, thrust her hand over the interview desk to greet the monk. Her eyes locked onto his and she saw his face for the first time, then his scars, his tattoos and his intimidating, muscular presence.

"The fuck you want?" growled the elderly, African American monk, ignoring the woman's hand and glaring at her, through his one good eye. His other eye was joined by a deep scar, from head to chin, straight through the centre, of that milky, dead eye.

A dread chill ran down her spine, but if ever there was a character worth interviewing, it was definitely him.

She stood frozen to the spot, hypnotised as it were, by that enigmatic man. She had to know everything, about this most unusual, inmate monk.

She clasped her hands together at her heart centre and bowed slightly at the waist, out of respect for the holy man.

"My apologies, in my excitement to meet with you, I forgot to knock and introduce myself. Please forgive me," said the journalist, gracefully tactful in her approach.

"Ah, excitement, yes. Excitement, can lead to many blunders and disasters, do be mindful of your excitement, especially around me," whispered the enigma of a man, dominating the room.

It was as if he were his surroundings, like the robes draped over his fierce, masculine frame.

She cleared her throat and stepped forward, with her head slightly bowed.

"Please forgive me, my name is Geeta and I seek permission to interview you," said the slenderly built, young woman.

"Shit! Ain't nothing to forgive! Sit down baby. We all good," said the broad monk, sat behind the desk.

"So, what's a fine-looking young woman like you, doing going to such great lengths to have me here? I know it ain't for my looks... Oh, and if you lie to me, even once, I'm out of here man. You dig?" said the monk, laughing.

The sharp and observant look in his eye, kept her from joining the laughter, as she sat motionless, totally awestruck by the old man.

She knew never to lie to this guy, this dangerous yet enchanting monk. She decided to drop any plans of deceit and be as direct as possible, lest her mind become his play thing.

"I want to know about San Diablo, as much as you can please. What do I call you?" asked Geeta, nervously.

The opposite of how she had planned things earlier that morning, when she first got the call from one of her fixers, announcing that they could arrange a small interview, with one of the legendary, American fighting monks of San Diablo. A myth she had thought, until today.

"Well, San Diablo is like, is like. It's the ashram, for the very worst of sinners," said the monk leaning in.

"Like me," he said laughing, his eye never leaving her face.

"An Ashram?" queried the journalist.

"Like a monastery, but for the very worst of criminals, those sentenced to death," said the huge older man, lighting a cigarette, enjoying the confusion on the journalists face.

"We turn sinners into saints at San Diablo. Through heart breaking sadhana, we cheerily take up our punishment and with great urgency, we work to undo the damage we have done, both to society and to our own karmic signature in the world," continued the monk, cryptically answering the unsolicited question, from the dumb struck reporter.

"I'm sorry, sadhana?" asked Geeta, returning her mind to the task at hand.

"Spiritual penance, practice and self-appointed austerities. You can think of it as exercise, that is if exercise could save your soul." laughed the huge monk and then from nowhere, silence. His face turned back to stone, amplifying his silence.

"What if anyone escapes the, erm, monastery?" asked Geeta, whispering and leaning forward over the table.

"Then our mother superior will command me and the trusted brethren, to drag their kicking and screaming asses back. They have a debt to pay! You dig?" answered the warrior monk. His black robes draped over his shoulder, revealing yet more tattoos and scars.

CHAPTER 1.

The air was dry and burning, from the arid stench of twenty shackled men. It stung at the eyes of the guards and filled the transport like a gas chamber. The smell of sweat, breath and fear, dripped from them, indeed the bus was rank with it, a primal terror that could shrink even these brutes.

Mr Hawshaw was the transport overseer. In all his twenty plus years, he had overseen the transport of every kind of criminal and every kind of man, or so he thought. He was no stranger to the hell of humanity, or the stench of murderers on his bus, neither was he a timid man by any measure, but this was no ordinary run and no ordinary bus full of animals.

Everyone was on edge, guards and inmates alike. All were deadly silent, more than silent, that silence had a weight to it, that silence had its own gravity that seemed to pull at the senses and pull you, straight to HIM.

The transport was an old Thomas school bus, painted black, that was one of the Wardens petty tricks, to the unfortunates, about to become his prisoners. He had his transports painted black to absorb the heat, he liked them to arrive already broken men. None of the windows opened for securities sake, but no air conditioning either, for spites sake.

The cab was separate from the rest of the bus. segregated by a dusty, flexi glass barrier, milky with scratches and old age. The driver was a mean looking old man, with a well lived in face, all wrinkled and shaped by decades of disdain, and his co- driver, an absolute monster of a man. A gigantic red neck, with keen, savage eyes, like a rattle snake with a gun, a man of gigantic proportions, the boss man.

His shotgun was always loaded and always pointed at the passengers, on his express bus to hell.

The inmates were shackled to their seats and each other, four in a row, five rows deep, five guards with guns ready flanked the inmates. One guard for every four prisoners. Behind them and totally separated from the rest of the transport, by electric mesh, was where they kept him, the special one.

Fully restrained and in a kneeling position. Five collars around his neck, tethered him by solid bars to the bus anchor points. His arms were chained out from his sides, they even put a shock belt around his waist, just in case.

All these restraints, and all these guards, just for him. If it were a different man with all the security, Mr

Hawshaw would be insulted, but no risks were being taken. Not with that tiger of a man.

He wasn't a particularly big guy, standing around 5′ 10″ with a lean, wiry frame, but this guy was all muscle and primal power, like a shark. While all around him were sweating and afraid, this one guy was calm, focused and terrifying.

Even the air around him, seemed to sense the electric danger of him, he didn't even look uncomfortable, even in that heat, even with that stink. That son of a bitch, looked like he was relaxing at the sauna.

He simply knelt there, still, calm, and deadly. The eyes on him were all you could see; sure, the cage was well lit, but that didn't matter, the intensity of his eyes masked his face, as if they could hide him and expose you. Expose you, to your very core.

"What's with the special case Boss?" trembled one of the thick set guards, through the cab window, visibly skittish and on edge.

"Papers say he's extremely dangerous, do not unshackle until base, Hell...it says here, in-case of a crash do not release, execute. Sounds like some big-time psycho to me boss, some god damn itchy looking mother fucker," asked the guard wistfully.

"Dangerous they say?" Snarled the boss man.

"Aren't they all boss?" ventured another guard.

"No, none of these assholes are, sure they act mean, but let me tell you Mitch, they all cry when their shits pushed in." laughed the Boss man.

The guards all laughed, a pleasant relief from the fear, but the laughter was hollow and short lived.

Mr Hawshaw spat on the ground, in front of the cab door and stared into the bus.

"They're all someone's bitch soon." he mocked. A smirk pulled at his face in sadistic satisfaction.

The prisoner in the cage began to laugh maniacally, as if privy to some secret joke, his eyes were fixed firmly on the boss man.

"That does not sound good" said the man in the cage, sarcastically. The guard closest to him, banged on the cage with his night stick.

"Shut your fucking dick hole, scum!" cussed the angry guard losing his composure in a pang of panic.

"Does not sound good at all" said the inmate, smiling now.

Smoke billowed out from the engine vents on the transport. Thick black, clouds of smoke, then the sound of dry engine parts destroying themselves against one another, filled the transporter. There was a loud Bang! Then the big old boy came to a stop.

"Shit call it in," shouted the boss man, glaring at the old driver.

"Calling it in boss," said the driver, trying hard not to look at the boss man.

"All eyes on our honoured guest here," ordered Mr Hawshaw, talking to the guards.

"Eyes on him boss." chirped the guards.

"Any bullshit and shoot him, shoot to kill" said the boss man, to the chorus of cocking shotguns.

Mr Hawshaw and the man's eyes locked across the hot and humid bus.

"You don't scare me bitch! so please, try something stupid...Bitch." spat the boss man, allowing his hate to get the better of him.

More raucous laughter came from the inmate, not a joyful infectious laugh, but the kind of laugh that mocks you, the kind that can freeze you, that kind of laugh that makes you do a stupid thing, a really stupid thing.

"Shut the fuck up, shut up!!!" one of the masked guards shouted, as he slammed the cage out of fear, with his night stick.

"Stop laughing bitch...shut up," spat the masked man, through trembling, frightened lips.

The other inmates, were freaked out and began shouting and pulling at their chains. The boss man blew on his whistle once and all became quiet, all except that caged animal, laughing louder and louder.

The formidable boss man, stepped out of the cab and into the main part of the bus. All eyes were on him, as he stepped menacingly down the bus, to the cage, to Him.

"I don't know what you did, to end up in this cage. I don't know what lousy choices got you to this place, all chained in a cage, like a common, filthy old dog, but if you don't, shut THE FUCK UP! Right now, I damn sure am gonna end your life right here!" Spat the enraged boss man.

He kept laughing though, even harder as if he was enjoying the wrath of others or the fear that he wrought.

"Have it your way" said the boss man, nodding to three masked guards.

The guards nodded back and slowly opened the cage, sticks in hand. There was a loud click, as the isolator turned off the shock fence. The inmate still laughed and laughed at them, then sticks were raised high, ready to do what brutes do best, try to kill what it was that made them afraid, to try and kill what it was that made them have that feeling of inadequacy.

"Wait...fry the Bastard!" said one of the masked guards.

The controller to the shock belt was on the front panel of the cage, a metal box with a big, red switch.

"When I press this, 20,000 volts are going to blast into you. You'll learn that I'm the boss man and that you're my prisoner," he snarled through clenched teeth, staring at the inmate, silent now, except his eyes.

The inmate took a deep breath in and turned his wrists towards himself, fingers in some kind of gesture.

" Fry him boss." one of the guards shouted in a panic.

His eyes rolled back, bringing focus and control to his incredible mind, switching his vegus nerve from auto function, to manual control. He bent his wrists towards himself and connected his fingers in a Mudra, one that gave him access to the flow of energy within him.

He felt the 20,000 volts from the shock belt and sent it all to the restraints at his feet, wrists and neck. In an instant he was free and in a blur of holy violence, he seized the opportunity to attack, without hesitation or doubt.

He was so fast, that you couldn't even register where he is, only where he was. It was as if light itself, could not keep up with him.

With a sickening crunch, he bought death to two of the guards, a high kick to the neck of one and a vicious chop to the neck of the other.

He grabbed the side arm gun from both cadavers and Bang, Bang, he shot the third guard twice in the forehead, the double tap. He looked to the boss man with a nod and shot one bullet, casually down the bus.

The bullet smashed into the boss man's shotgun and disabled the firearm completely. The uncaged man, dropped the two service revolvers to the ground and stepped forward, towards the big man.

Bang, Bang, Bang...The Boss man fired his revolver. A much bigger gun than the other guards, a magnum, a modified and customised agent of death. He squose off three rounds, but they hit nothing but air.

"That's three," said the prisoner.

BANG, BANG, again both shots missed their mark.

"That's five." mocked the inmate with a smile.

"Only one left, Mr Boss Man." The man's smooth British accent was frightening by itself, it was as if the speaker was the authority above you. It made you feel less somehow, with its aggressively refined tone and ability to speak to the soul.

The message, that this speaker was above you, that this speaker, was dangerously intellectual and that when words are exhausted, action will follow.

He strode past the stunned boss man, down to the lower part of the bus, where the other inmates cowered as far away, as their restraints would allow.

The remaining two guards, guns trembling in their hands, stood wide legged and braced themselves for what could happen next. If the coin of fate would land favourably or not, did not matter to them, only their unwavering duty to the warden.

"Only one shot left old boy...be a shame for you to die with no bullets, wouldn't you agree?" asked the enigmatic prisoner.

 Hawshaw lowered his gun and motioned to the guards to lower their weapons too.

Sirens began making their presence known, way off in the desert void. The man strode towards the inmates, he stopped at the end of the row and looked down on their cowering forms, trying to scramble away.

 "Time for your freedom gentlemen" he said, breaking their chains with his bare hands.

 "Contrary to all the evidence presented, you chaps, will be quite useful after all." he said, smiling as if amused by them. He stepped back and motioned for them to get up.

 "Whoa there fellow, hang on a God damn minute" said the boss man, recovering from the shock of violence.

 He pressed his revolver to the back of the man's head and faster than a blink, the man turned around and jammed the guns hammer with his thumb.

 "How very disappointing, I was hoping to" began the man. He turned the gun around, disarming the boss man and finished the big supervisor, with his own last bullet, straight through the forehead.

"Let you live." he continued, with a faux deep sigh.

The two remaining guards yanked their shot guns up to their shoulders, ready to gun down this savage, this Bastard that murdered their colleagues and boss.

The panicked and exhausted inmates wasted no time, as they rushed into the guards, desperate to get off that vehicle of despair.

Bang, Bang, Click, Pump, Bang, three inmates hit the deck, blood pouring from their chests and abdomens. The guards were quickly subdued and beaten to death, by those seventeen desperate, brutal men.

The man from the cage grabbed one inmate by the shoulder, breaking the prisoner from his blood lust.

"Spot on, now tool up and fuck off," growled the enigma of a man. The inmate paused a moment, hypnotised by the man's burning eyes.

"Now! move it, move it, move it, go! Go! Go!" Roared the mysterious man.

They scrambled at what weapons they could grab and forced the cab open, ripping the old driver to pieces in a frenzy of barbarism.

"Just a moment chaps. Don't get caught," he said, then smiled at them in approval as they turned back, they did not smile or understand, but he smiled all the same, like it was all part of his plan. Part of some sick game, played with blood, and balls. He watched until all the inmates had turned away.

One inmate, a dry, weasel looking man, turned round and saw a gun go off and a body drop.

"Don't blame Ya guy, its better n what they'd do to Ya fur this, that's fur sure." He said, sniffing hard at a fake tear.

"My fucking hero" he mocked, rubbing his eyes as if crying.

"What was that?" demanded a tall, dark, and chubby prisoner.

"He's killed himself Bubba, you dumb son of a bitch! He's praps the only man who can." said Rufus coldly.

"C'mon, let's move it girls, it'll be high noon soon. Gotta git to the shade, gotta hide! C'mon." said another inmate, a vicious looking old Nazi man, with a swastika tattoo on his right cheek and the number 88 on the other.

"Bring the Nigger," said the vial racist.

"Fuck you, white boy!" Shouted Bubba, disgusted by the old supremist.

"Stop fucking around! Let's move," said another, a smaller white guy. He looked like an accountant, and way out of place with these dregs.

"Better muzzle that shit honkey," hissed Bubba angrily.

Slap! The small guy slapped Bubba so hard across his face, that the big man fell over hard, in the hot sand.

"I said move! One gets caught and we're all fucked, now move!" hissed the man, angrily.

Bubba got up, glaring at the supremist, with utter hate in his eyes.

"For now." he said viciously.

San Diablo, the devils haven.

CHAPTER 2.

The screech of speeding cars and sirens, became feinter and feinter the further they ran. In the distance what looked like a window, reflecting in the bright desert sun, could be made out.

"Keep going, head that way, we can regroup, rest and have a minute to think, move it, for fuck's sake, keep moving," said the small man, urgently.

"Throw out your weapons and come out with your hands up" a voice announced through a mega phone. No reply. A beep echoed out, as the officer pressed the vox again "you are surrounded, throw out your weapons" repeated the voice.

Prison personnel and armed special police, dressed in black, tactical riot gear and armed with semi-automatic assault rifles, swarmed the bus. Red laser beams, dotted this way and that, as the agents moved in.

The anxiety was palpable among them, this was important, no room for error. The transport guards were complacent, a mistake not to be repeated by these guys, everything by the number, no show boating.

"Get on the floor, hands by your heads...we are coming in" said the voice on the vox.

Nobody was moving on the bus, just bodies and blood. The troopers surrounding the bus, stepped cautiously closer and closer, guns at the ready, on the shoulder, loaded.

" Ready, smash." ordered the commander.

Two windows smashed on the side of the bus, the inside of the transporter, was filled with red dots as the first wave, of the scout and assess team entered.

"Clear! Looks like a blood bath, what the heck happened in here?" said one of the spectre like troops.

"Proceed with extreme caution! Rico?" said an officer.

One of the troops snapped to attention.

"Take your team and check it out, I need a count" said the officer, obviously InCharge.

"Yes Sir" chipped Rico, from behind his mask and respirator.

Three agents, donned in black body armour and respirators, slowly, cautiously, entered the bus.

"Over watch formation," barked commander Rico.

"Just like Fallujah huh Sir?" one trooper added to the silence, her gravelled voice of a veteran, fit the gloom perfectly.

"Yeah, I hear that...Sophia...what have we got here?" said Rico.

"Looks like nine fatalities Sir, five guards, four inmates. Looks like a goddamn ambush to me, but I can't find any trace of the assailants," reported Sophia.

Commander Rico handpicked, his elite team of the absolute best active soldiers, he could get. The fact that they were women, made him the butt of many jokes with the old boys. That is, until he'd click his fingers and his team would kick ass. Then the laughter would stop, it always did.

These were his own elite guards, the very best.

"Sharky, check vitals." he barked at another trooper.

"Sir, we got a live one, but he's fading fast," reported agent Sharky.

"Medic team, on me!" shouted commander Rico, and in a flash, a medic team was in the bus.

"What happened here?" asked the medic team leader, trying hard not to breathe in through the stench of the bus.

"What happened here is we got one, semi alive witness and seventeen of the most dangerous and depraved men alive, out of their chains" said commander Rico, stepping to pick up the broken shackles on the floor.

"What a mess." he whispered.

" Now it's your mess, Rico" said a tall man in a black suit, shot vest and mirrored sunglasses. An ear piece, buzzed orders in his ears.

He was a CIA and a high up one too.

"Sir, officer on board!" roared the agent, snapping to a smart salute.

Ricos team snapped to attention, saluting the tall man.

"At ease! medic?" said the tall man, getting the medic teams attention.

"Sir" responded the team leader, allowing as much attention as he could spare, while administering first aid to the downed inmate. The other two medics were administering pain killers, via a canular in the mans blooded left hand.

"I need this man taking to the prison infirmary, a helicopter is on route. He is to be fully restrained and sedated at all times, until I say otherwise. Clear?" asked the faceless CIA man.

"Clear sir." chirped the commander, through gritted teeth.

"Rico, I have a new task for you, pursue and capture our escapees, kill if you must," said the agent.

"Sir, yes Sir" returned Rico, smiling. His kind of mission at last.

"Come with me Rico" said the agent, removing his ear piece, and walking away from the others, in a hushed, pressed tone.

"This is a big fucking deal Rico, one of these men is not like any others. He's a high-level target. Extremely well trained and extremely dangerous. Look, if he gets away, everything we have worked for goes down the shitter and that means Me, You and Your, ah men, are we clear?" asked the CIA man.

"Eye Sir clear" hissed Rico.

The CIA special agent, grabbed hold of Ricos arm.

"Take two support teams, and stay in contact. He cannot get away, he has, shall we say, some valuable data and skills. Valuable to uncle Sam, but also, to the fucking Kasaks," said the superior.

"Eye Sir, Alpha team on me!" ordered Rico, as he pressed the radio comms on his shoulder.

"Hudson, Suarez, move your teams out on me. Let's roll" ordered Rico, he turned back to the agent.

"I'll have your canary back in time to sing, Sir." He said firmly with a nod.

"God speed commander, stop for nothing." said the tall agent, turning away.

The mysterious special agent, opened the cab door and

stepped into the gore chamber, where the driver breathed his last breath. Blood and gore were splattered everywhere.

A pair, of half smashed mirrored sunglasses swung on the steering wheel. The radio speaker though smashed, was still crackling and buzzing to the gloom.

The CIA man agent Malone, checked over his shoulder, double checking if anyone had eyes on him. He pulled a small, silver memory stick, from what looked like a cigarette tin and inserted it with a click, into the centre of the steering wheel, into a secret docking port.

The memory stick flashed, from a red light to green in a matter of seconds. He checked over his shoulder again, then put the memory stick back in the cigarette tin.

Malone exited the bus, dusting his jacket with the flat of his hand.

"Ok everyone, gather round. I, am special agent Malone of the CIA. We have a situation here people," he bellowed, to the remaining teams of specialists.

"We have, somewhere out there, seventeen escaped prisoners, but only one of them is the target. The rest can die on the sand, or come home to our dear warden. One of them however, our man, is an extremely dangerous and valuable individual. All we can say, is that he is a

Brit, around five foot ten, Caucasian, brown eyes, with mousey hair." He held up a photograph of the man to the crowd.

"He assassinated a senator and his entire security detail, in a rally in Tulsa. Did I mention he was unarmed? Unarmed and killed twenty-five secret service personal and a God damned senator. All in ninety-seven seconds, I shit you not. He was kept in the cage, sedated and fully restrained. Only he aint there now, another inmate is though, in his jumpsuit. He was found in his place, with half his face shot off," said Malone.

He looked every one of those assembled in the eye.

"He's fucking with us, so let's show him who he's fucking with. Commander Rico and his teams, are tracking our walkers. I need blow by blow reports and the files on all those on that bus, transcript of the driver's coms with base, and I need them now!" snapped Malone, with a clap of his hands.

A long black car with tinted windows, pulled up alongside the bus.

Another tall, athletic man in a black suit and sunglasses, got out of the passenger side and opened the rear door of the car, and spoke into his wrist.

Agent Malone pressed his ear piece, and listened with the kind of concentration, that eludes normal men.

"We will be operating from the warden's office, you have ninety minutes to hand me your reports," announced Malone.

The agent turned and walked towards the car; the other faceless agent moved sideways, out of his way, allowing a glimpse into the spy car.

A screen full of mugshots, of all the inmates was visible for a moment, then was obscured again, by the frame of Special agent Malone.

The helicopter touched down, sending the desert dust everywhere. It was a large, twin motor sea knight helicopter, commandeered by this very special prison, for evacuation and air ambulance.

The medic team, sprinted to the sliding door with their injured charge on a stretcher.

"Oh, and I want that man able to talk! Interviewed and in a cell by the end of the day, are we clear?" barked Malone menacingly, over the medic team leaders shoulder radio.

The aggressively smooth voice of agent Malone, echoed in all the ear pieces, of the medic team.

"Roger Sir, he'll sing today," returned the medic.

The gurney was locked in place, with the prisoner fully strapped to it.

"Ok! Let's go, let's go," radioed the medic to the Sea king crew. The big Sea king helicopter, threw dust and sand out like an explosion of power, and in an instant it was airborne.

"Sir!" shouted the tracker from team Gamma, a short but powerfully built, Latino man in his late twenties. Tattoos snaked up his neck and hands, an Ex-gang banger. A tracker from MS18 turned Law man, to make right all his wrongs.

Officer Delgado was a much-respected law man. Like most of the new personnel assigned to Malone, an Ex-con turned law enforcer.

"Sir!" repeated Delgado urgently.

Rico ran on his position.

"Tracks here Sir, seventeen on foot, all ran this way.
There was a fight here" Delgado said squatting down and
pointing, to some new tracks.

 Existing in the past, as he relived the escape, setting his
mind to that of the escapees.

 "Two of them, one big guy," he motioned to the deep,
large foot prints of Bubba.

"He got slammed by an old Gringo here," said first tracker Delgado, lifting a long, crinkly grey hair between his thumb and fore finger.

He shuffled a little further, examining new foot prints.

"One of them stopped the fight here and, and" his eyes darted around the ground, for any other clues left behind, in the moving desert sand.

"And here, south, south west," said Delgado. He moved faster, stooping to the ground.

"They caught up with the rest here," said the tracker, standing up, head on a swivel.

"This way," said the stout tracker, pointing the way.

"Saddle up," shouted Rico.

He gestured by circling the air, that it was time.

"Teams Beta and Gamma follow us" said Rico, Delgado faced commander Rico.

"You're with me," said Rico lifting his head towards the three teams, of elite soldiers.

"Roll out." ordered the commander.

Alpha team consisted of Commander Rico, Delgado, Sophia and Sharky with O'Hara, Alpha team, Ricos personnel guard. These three women were hardened veterans of many wars and campaigns.

Sophia, the tallest of the trio, stood at 5'10". Long, thick black hair, pale skin and an athletic physique, in her late twenties.

Sharky was a little shorter, at 5' 8", mean, piercing brown eyes, and a lean, lithe frame. Her face was covered in tribal scarring. A slightly older women in her thirties, but age hadn't slowed her down one bit. A fierce, terrifying, lion of a woman, and of course O'Hara, the shortest of the three.

Her short red hair was the colour of fire and her wide, chiselled jaw, sat a top of a neck like a pit bull.

A powerhouse of a women, muscular, tense, and deadly.

Alpha team rode out on desert bikes, Rico, Delgado, Sophia, Sharky and O'Hara at the rear.

Team Beta, in an armoured Hummer, consisted of a team of five.

Team Gamma, now a member down, consisted of four, in a personnel carrier, forward Opps, mobile centre, a lenco bear cat.

A tricked out and supped up, old swat carrier.

The inmates ran faster than they knew they could, hearts almost bursting from their chests.

The old Nazi man Rufus, dropped to the ground gasping and clutching at his chest.

The hot desert air, was like fire in his lungs. He screamed for the help, that he wished he could muster, in his dry and panicked throat.

He rolled on his back holding his chest, praying at the end, to a god he had forsaken.

The old man opened his eyes for the last time and gazed in horror, at his last sight. To be the witness of his god's response, to years of blasphemy, the enormous boot of Bubba. The huge black man, stamped on the old Nazi, over and over again. Crushing the Nazis skull, against the hot Nevada sand.

Bubba, hands on knees, powered gulps of air into his gigantic chest.

"Sooner, gasp, than I thought" gasped the African American inmate.

A panic washed over him, as he caught his breath. Eyes darting around the blank desert plain, searching for the others. He turned frantically on the spot, trying desperately to find a way out of that dust bowl, back to the others. His only hope for survival.

He noticed through dry, punished eyes, a shimmering reflection of the sun on glass.

Empowered by a combination of hope and despair in equal measure, he took to his feet again, one more push, one more burst of energetic tenacity, to the illusion of safety.

The others just kept going, until eventually, the glimmer of hope became un obscured. The flash of the sun reflecting on glass, their only chance of salvation, came into view.

An RV parked next to what looked like, an abandoned mine entrance. A large wooden shack, cobbled together, by miners not carpenters. A Dusty and dilapidated old structure, but it looked like a castle to those desperate men.

The escaped inmates charged towards the big shiny recreation vehicle, with renewed vigour and hope. The sliding side door was already open, so in they charged, like animals at the trough.

There was no one in the vehicle, it was abandoned. One of the men tore open the refrigerator, in a blast of action.

"Beer!" he exclaimed with utter delight. Trembling, he grabbed at one, but was hastily pushed aside, by this swathe of men, mad with thirst and pain.

"Woo, Woo" the accountant looking man, called out in excitement.

"We don't know who was here, how many, or how long before the police will be here. We need a plan! You!" he pointed to a big, red, panting inmate, draining a can, fresh from the refrigerator.

"Get some boys and check that place out, must be something good in there, for this to be here. Rest of you, get supplies," ordered the man.

"Who the fuck put you in charge of this here outfit? Who the hell d'ya think you are?" snapped a big old white boy, a six foot three, mean Hill billy, with a shot gun pointed at the smaller man.

The smaller inmate, calmly pushed the barrel to one side with his finger and looked up to the giant heap, of hair and sweat. Then Bang!!!

The smaller guy jumped up and headbutted the giant, cutting his eyebrow open and sending the big man down.

He took the firearm, with a snap.

"Because looking at you gaggle, of dumb looking sons of bitches gathered here, I'd say I'm the only one here, with even a hope for a plan. Now do as I fucking say and we might even get out of this bastard alive. You with me?" said the shorter inmate, bigger somehow.

He turned towards the assembly of men.

"Well, are you?" he asked.

"What do they call you mister?" enquired one of the men.

"I'm Hannibal, and I got us a plan," smiled Hannibal. The other inmates reluctantly followed him, off the recreation vehicle, towards the old shack building.

"What is this place? asked one convict, a well-built white man, with a clean-shaven head and dark moustache.

He had the same tattoo on his face as Rufas, the numbers 88 on one side of his neck and the double thunder bolt insignia, of the Nazi SS.

"And where the fuck, is my sweet white brother? Bet one of these fucking spooks got to him" he furthered, while walking to the centre. Strutting and sticking his chest out, gesturing aggressively to the group in general.

"Everybody just chill THE FUCK OUT! they will be here any time now, and I ain't wasting this chance to escape. We won't get another!" Said Hannibal, turning on the spot to hold the attention, of each of those spent, exhausted and dangerous men.

"The only chance of getting out of this fucking desert and back to the world, is by pulling in for now, OR, we could play pin the Red neck on the Nigger and see how far that gets us." continued Hannibal, commanding the space brilliantly, to the laughter of most of those, desperate and exhausted men.

These escapees, had no desire for the chains of captivity, especially in that place.

San Diablo, the devils haven.

CHAPTER 3.

They had all heard rumours about the place of course,
but they had dismissed them as rumours and bullshit, but
there they were, escaping the transport bus that would

have delivered them all to hell, to deliver them there, to San Diablo, the Devils prison.

They, would say a lot about that place, whoever they, are. No one ever really knows who they really are, but they say San Diablo is a living hell.

They say that, one minute you're asleep and Boom, next thing, you're waking up in shackles and in a whole world of shit. The prison doctor would pronounce you dead to the world.

Sure, they'd tell your family it was suicide, or gang related, or some other bullshit, but to the world you'd be dead and you'd disappear from heart and memory and enter into Hell. The Devils own prison, where experiments were carried out on those men, of guilt and shame.

They say that to even get a toilet seat, or a mattress you'd have to volunteer to the program. They couldn't do it without your signature, without your consent. Why he'd heard, that they were into some real dark shit there. Like summoning demons' kind of dark.

A place where an inmate becomes no more than a slave. They had all heard these stories and then some.

None of them would go there, they would rather die first, the more traditional way to descend into Hades, not like that, that would be living in Hell and then dying, only for sure to return, but right then it was the fire in their bellies.

 The fear of the place gave them the strength to go on, the power to endure and the audacity to hope, where hope was forbidden.

"Looks like an old mine, there's some stairs going down," one of the Latino prisoners ventured.

 "Well go and check it out, Chieco" mocked the big Nazi, in a fake Mexican accent, just daring the man to hit him.

 "Ci Senjor" returned the Latino man, spitting on the floor in front of the big Nazi.

 The other five white inmates, gravitated towards him, likes wolfs to their Alpha, waiting for his call to action.

 Although these were inmates from all over America, they were all brothers of the same family, the Nazi Brotherhood, the 88-tattoo visible on all of them.

"I've got a good job for you brothers," said Hannibal, advancing towards the group of convicts. A gang is good, a gang is cohesive and a gang he could use.

The brothers gathered around the much smaller man.

The sea knight roared in the air, filling an endless sky with the sound of twin rotors, singing like thunder. "Can't this crate go any faster?" panicked the chief medic.

"We are losing him!" he added, while he and his team fought desperately, to keep the inmate from flatlining.

"Shit" ... squeaked one of the medics, as the pulse read out transitioned from the rhythmic beat of a functioning heart, to the single long beep of the flatline.

"He's gone again," shouted one medic.

The prisoner's jumpsuit was torn open and cut wide, his taut, bloodied chest was exposed and his arms and legs, were strapped to the gurney.

Multiple drip feeds administered hormones, painkillers and steroids, all to make him alive enough for the interview. Then his organs would be removed from him, alive or dead, then sold to the hospitals, or worse than that, he could be used in a death ceremony.

A brutal tradition in San Diablo, where an inmate, who has become useless and weak, not strong enough for the task, was stomped to death at the boots of the warden's personal guard, for sport.

The raw, blooded lump of meat in a jumpsuit, would be dragged anti clockwise, thirty-three times around the yard perimeter fence, this is done to trap the soul of the inmate forever in that hell and to discipline those who might dare to revolt.

The remains were hung up high, for a day and a night as a statement of dominion, until it was cremated and stored.

"Fuck" exclaimed the medic.

The noise of a stopped heart on the monitor, filled the chopper and seemed to drown out the din of the rotors.

"Clear" he continued, defribulator clasped in his hands.

BOO, BUMP, the man's body lurched and dropped.

"C'mon, C'mon," BOOMP, another lurch. Nothing, but the low continuous beep of the monitor.

"Clear" BOO, BOOMP, BEEP, ...BEEP...BEEP.

"Come on you ugly bastard, come on," BEEP...BEEP...

"Fading, blood pressure dropping" sounded a medic, caught in the grip of panic.

"Bump up the adrenaline... 50 ccs, cut off the painkillers," barked the Chief medic, pumping a respirator to keep the man alive.

A third medic hammered a fist, on the man's chest. They were in the clutches of desperation, after all who wants to fail the Boss? Especially that Boss.

"Malones going to have our balls! Stay with us, you asshole! Long enough till we get you there, you can die only, when they're done with you. Stay with us!!" he screamed. He slapped the prisoner across the cheeks, half in hate and half in loathing.

Surrounded by chain link fencing, the enormous facility came into view, through the double opening in the Sea Knight helicopter.

The perimeter was a large circle of electrified chain link fences, easily five miles across. Monitored at all times by security cameras, check points and armed guards, with dogs, guns and a sadistic disposition.

An outpost of Hell, in the unforgiving Nevada desert.

The middle of nowhere, the ideal setting for that theatre of despair and depravation.

Within the perimeter fence, away from any of the unpleasantness, were the visitor's quarters, and their facilities, barracks, gym, and mess hall. To the North was the intake yard, where the Devils guests, are processed.

In the centre of the complex, are three unusual buildings, the first one, a large Pentagon, 3.3 miles across and 35 feet wide. Inside this megalithic structure, is another Pentagon building, hollow as the last, but oriented at ninety degrees from the first.

They were the main prison holding facilities with the compliant inmates, those willing to follow the guards will totally, were housed. While the smaller of the two buildings, housed those waiting to submit. The areas between the buildings, were fenced off into sections, by the same electric fencing and coils of shiny, cruel, razor wire, were used for segregation, ceremonies and to facilitate the breaking of an inmate, in the baking Climate of the hot desert.

Dead centre, in the middle of the second Pentagon, was a complete Pentagon building. This was where the experiments happened, and the bodies were burned, the middle of Hell on earth. The razor wires reflection, was blinding in the unsheltered desert sand.

"Strap in and shut up" commanded a tall member of the flight crew.

"We're going in." he continued.

The medical team, strapped in and held onto whatever they could grab. The pilot radioed in to the control tower.

"Black knight, black knight, requesting landing clearance, over," CLICK, a pause filled the cabin of the old boy, then.

"Tower two to Black Knight. Infirmary team on standby. Clear to land. Over."

The pilot and co-pilot, both wore the black uniform of the considerable prison security detail. Both had tinted, full face visors and both were armed with a side arm gun, along with two M16 assault rifles, strapped in place above them in the cockpit.

They looked at each other and nodded, both men silently smirked to each other.

The large Sea knight helicopter, suddenly dropped 20 feet in the air and rose back again, to its original point of altitude, a practical joke from the crew.

One of the medics fell backwards, arms flailing, trying desperately not to fall to his end. He fell to his back, rolling and clutching out to anything that would help him survive.

Instinct took over for medical officer Harris, as he flung his arm, one last time, into the well of fortune. He grabbed a loose strap buckle in the rush, and somehow it wrapped itself around, lucky Harris's wrist. His body snapped to, at the end of the strap, dangling and screaming in mid-air.

The screams of terror, were drowned out by the laughter of the flight crew.

"Y'all hang in there, we experiencing a little turbulence," roared the crew men, sadistically and sarcastically.

The chopper came closer and closer to the prison, descending into the home of the damned, San Diablo.

Officer Harris was fully in the grip of panic. He scrambled wildly at the strap, one hand, then the other, then, a POP sound happened as he got to the top of his climb. Harris started to fall, then he stopped, and scrambled up onto the ledge of the Sea knight.

His luck, fully spent, and eyes open wide. He looked up to see the gurney, prisoner and all, rolling heavily towards him.

"Jesus save me," were his last words before the screaming started, but not for long.

"Holy shit, land it, land it!" yelled the chief medic, enraged and red with wrath.

"We Gotta land on the pad, you know that," chuckled the pilot.

"You killed him, you son of a ...," snapped the medic, until he was cut off by the pilot.

"Careful son, remember who you're talking to! You land locked pussies, should have strapped up and that's the end of it, clear?" asked the pilot.

No response from the team leader, violently shaking in rage.

"I said clear?!" barked the pilot, menace in his voice.

"Clear sir," answered the shaking man, to the delight of the pilot, sadistically laughing at the man's indignation.

The two remaining medics, looked knowingly at each other. They didn't speak, they didn't have to, their eyes did all the talking, and those eyes said murder, those eyes said revenge and those eyes said...

"Now!"

Both men drew at their personal side arms, and pulled up from their hips. The crew immediately reacted and drew their weapons. In a flash, the chief medic shot first, straight into the pilots back.

The bullet went through the chair, through him and into the flight controls, sending electric sparks into the helicopter's cockpit.

The flight technician shot next, hitting the head medic in the abdomen, but not killing him. Only to be shot in the face, by the wounded man.

The co-pilot unbuckled, and standing, squose off a full magazine into the belly of the Sea knight. He'd killed them both, but the victory, as they often times are, was short lived. The big old bird crashed into the prison intake yard, with smoke billowing out of its engine.

The pilot moaned and threw the pile, of body parts and debris, from on top of him, then staggered to his feet.

Ears ringing and bleeding, he allowed himself a laugh and a woohoo! Then a familiar smell hit his nose and his eyes widened, in the realisation of oblivion. High octain fuel, was leaking in from everywhere and then, in a flash, BOOM! The giant bird exploded like an atom bomb.

The explosion scattered parts of the chopper and the pilot, all over the prison.

The group of Neo Nazis, sprinted out of the mine and dashed towards the RV.

The Alpha of the group, empowered by the others had become driven by expectation. The hopes of his brothers and their expectations of him, elevated his mind to that of a leader. He sped to the driver side and swung the door open.

The others scrambled aboard, carrying weapons and supplies of water and beer, found in the mine entrance lockers.

They all boarded, with doors slamming shut as the RV pealed out, into the void of the Nevada desert.

Hannibal dashed back into the shack, to the mine opening. The entrance was at least 8 feet wide by 7-feet high. A dangerous looking erection if ever there was one.

Rudimentary lights fed from a gas generator, and led off down into the gloom.

There were signs that the mine had been used recently. The inmates had already found water, some candy, beer and weapons, but not a soul was there. Even spilt coffee on the small table, in the middle space of the old shack. Still warm, as if the mine was evacuated in a hurry, as though the miners working there, ran with Hell at their heels.

"Hey!" growled a stocky, young and heavily tattooed Latino prisoner, to Hannibal.

"So, where are they Gringo? Something scared them bad, eh?" asked the tattooed gangster.

The other inmates looked around at each other knowingly, then at Hannibal.

"They saw us coming and got spooked, probably got cameras all over the desert," replied Hannibal casually to the room.

"Yeah, so why cameras, why they need cameras here, eh, clever man?" questioned another.

"Well for a start, this is an illegal mine. Look around you man," Hannibal again turned his attention to the room.

"Listen up, we have no clue as to what's down there, but we know what's, out there," motioning to the shack door.

"When they get here, and they will. All they will find, will be foot prints in the sand and vehicle tracks leading off," explained Hannibal.

"So," barked another Latino man, small, wirey, and vicious looking.

"So," continued Hannibal.

"So, they will fucking follow that! they gonna think someone bust us out, and they gonna think we met them here, they'll look around, find the tracks then fuck off following the RV," do you get that huh? Fucking think man!" roared Hannibal, pinching his nose in frustration.

"You're one smart, sweet, mother fucker, Hannibal. so, we just hide out and wait for them fools to ghost? Man, I love that shit," offered one of the three, African American prisoners, clapping his hand on another.

"We got food, we got drink and we got guns, so let's all just shut up and wait, can we all do that?" said Hannibal, in a condescending tone, smiling at the stocky Latino man.

"I don't like it, don't feel good to me man," said the man, he kissed his fingers and made the sign of the cross.

"You scared Chieco?" mocked one of the black inmates.

" Ci, because I'm smart, they are more worst things than these law men," said the Latin gangster.

"Oh, yeah like what?" returned the inmate, "what's worse than those pigs?"

"Like the warden, you know who he is essay?" asked the Latino man, "El Diablo!" he continued, holding the gaze of the inmate.

"Ok, keep it brave, we just have to be patient and I don't want to hear no more of that Devil crap either, stick to the god damned plan!" whispered Hannibal, hushing the group.

San Diablo, the devils haven.

CHAPTER 4.

The warden of course, had the best room of the house. Dark mahogany panelled walls, each adorned with macabre art. Original illustrations from antiquity depicting crime, punishment and warning posters. All showing, from one degree to another, either the torture, or execution of prisoners throughout the ages.

Above the large, thick oak door, was hung the very axe that dispatched William Wallace of Scotland. Above his large, sloped windows, the noose of Guy Fawks of England, and on his desk, the very nails that crucified the Nazrine. Next to them, a Japanese lamp, made from the tattooed skin, of an executed Yakuza daimyo.

The door, was opposite the window wall facing south, positioned thus by the warden, to obscure the vision of those entering the room. He could see them, but they could never fully see him, on account of the blinding Nevada sun.

The large Mahogony desk, sat 6 feet from the window and exactly 12 feet from the door, in the centre of the room hung a crystal chandelier, flanked and surrounded, by exquisite ceiling murals, a macabre scene, straight out of Miltons paradise lost. Lining the walls above head height, hunting trophies, the stuffed and mounted heads, of large game animals. Lions, Bears, and an elephant's foot umbrella stand, a Gorillas hand, even a panda skin rug.

All killed to amuse him and it still amused him. When he'd look, as he did from time to time, the pleasure that he would get from just looking at them, was nearly as euphoric, as the moment he killed them.

The room was filled with the sickly-sweet aroma of fine Cuban cigars, and there he sat. In front of the window, in a high-backed chesterfield arm chair, upholstered in Rhino leather, studded with gold and diamonds. Like a king on his throne. The apex predator, El Diablo, sat rage stricken, as if paralysed with wrath.

A much shorter man than you'd imagine for one so powerful, standing at four feet seven inches. He was a shorter man that never looked small, his presence was that of a much bigger man, than the one sat in that decadent room.

He had a large frame, a very, large frame. Years of opulent living hung around his body, like a seal skin body suit. His round face had small, sharp features, with narrow, mean eyes.

He wore a sweat and blood-stained linen suit; a sweat transparent white shirt and a white Panama hat, that he frequently misused as a fan, before thrusting it back onto his dank, swollen head.

He wore a big golden watch, on one enormous wrist and multiple thick gold chains, around the other. Both wrists were studded with blood diamonds, from his plunderous adventures in Africa.

The warden snapped out a handkerchief from his breast pocket, and wiped thick rivers of sweat, from one side, of his blotchy pale white face, to the other. He sat bolt upright in the chair; hands capped over the arm rest. He tipped his head back and closed his mean, little eyes.

"What is your bidding my master?" he uttered in a deep, bestial voice. The mural above him began to move and change shape.

A black car, accelerated towards, the Sea knight crash site.

Green augmented data, appeared and disappeared on the inside windscreen, of the CIA car along with images taken from the prison security footage. "Approaching landing zone of our bogey sir," announced the agent, driving the sleek SUV.

"I want full footage from the descent of the inmate, to present time, from all cameras in this section," ordered agent Malone, to the agent in the passenger seat operating multiple screens at once.

Malone turned his attention to an open dossier, documents and photographs bound in a green card folder, with the words 'TOP SECRET', stamped in bold red ink, across both sides. On a top corner, on the file index tab, bore the word, RUDRA.

The car slid to a stop, close to the projected site of the inmate, as calculated by Jeffries, the agent in the passenger seat. The brains of the three-man army, a genius by most standards and a hard bastard, by all standards.

The three agents, rose from the car and put on their CIA issue sunglasses, with mechanical synchronicity. They strode a few paces, until Jeffress, suddenly stopped and looked up. Agent Malone and agent Stirling, the driver, stopped almost at once behind him, either side. The two agents turned their heads, to silently look at the incredible agent, calculating the path they should tread.

Agent Jeffries closed his eyes, just for a moment.

His eyes snapped open, wide with realisation. Jeffress raised his right arm; exposing a holstered semiautomatic, the Israeli Galli ace, Jeffries personal side arm. He pointed to a small pile of twisted shrapnel, a short way off.

"There, the bed landed there, but he's not going to be there, sir." said Jeffries.

"Oh" enquired Malone.

"New data from helicopter feed, Delta. He jumped from the gurney and clung to the helicopter. The crash obscured any image being captured, but he's here sir, hiding." said Jeffries, with a face like granite.

"Son of a bitch! He's loose," said Malone, turning to Jeffries.

"Can you enhance the image from the crash?" Asked Malone.

"It will take some time." answered the agent.

"How much time?" snapped Malone impatiently.

"Sir, I'll need at least 3 hours to overlap and triangulate." began Jeffries.

"We can only spare one," interrupted Malone, holding a hand up.

"You're the genius, make it happen." said Malone, as smooth as silk.

"Yes sir." returned Jeffries, already getting in the car to his tech.

"Stirling" said agent Malone, turning to the driver.

"I need the name of all inmates, within eye shot of here and arrange interviews today," ordered Malone, mechanically.

"As you command," replied agent Stirling, flatly.

"I think it's time for me to speak to this warden, there's something wrong here, something fucked up." he paused, looking up at a guard tower.

"Stay frosty, and trust no one here. Rendezvous on my location in one hour." said Malone looking at the agent enthusiastically enhancing the crash footage.

"One hour," he said firmly.

Malone left the other two men in the car and motioned to a guard standing nearby, the guard ambled over to the agent.

"What" spat the man.

Malone slapped him clean off his feet.

"Don't you ever speak to me like that again, you hear me?" screamed Malone, absolutely livid.

The guard hurried to his feet, scowling back at him, WHACK! He slapped him again across the face, harder this time.

"Take me to the warden, and don't you ever eye ball me either," hissed Malone, adjusting his tie.

Other guards gathered round, some with weapons drawn. One, foolishly pointed his shotgun at the agent.

Malone was fast, deadly fast. Before any of them could even think or react, the big agent snatched the heavy fire arm off the man and crashed it butt first into his face, sending the guard to the floor, blood pouring from a broken jaw.

"And no one, and I do mean no one, pulls a gun on me, because I might not be in such a jolly mood next time." grunted Malone.

He unloaded the gun, sending shells onto the prison yard floor and threw the weapon, in disgust, back at the man.

The first guard stood mouth open, gauping in disbelief at what he had witnessed.

"Well," said Malone, forcibly closing the man's chin with a chilling click, "shall we?"

The guard, holding his face, tipped his head motioning for the agent to follow him.

"This way," mumbled the guard, holding tears back. 'WHACK! The guard fell harder that time, face first onto the ground.

"It's this way, SIR," said Malone, indignantly "you really must work on your manners."

Malone leaned in close to the downed man, "it might save your life," he whispered, menacingly

"Yes SIR," responded the guard, barely able to stand.

"You there," snapped Malone to a second guard. The man nervously saluted the agent and stepped forward.

"Sir yes sir," responded the guard. Malone saluted the man back.

"At ease." snapped Malone, smiling.

The man almost crumpled into a heap, out of relief.

"Take me to the warden," ordered Malone.

"Yes sir" trembled the guard, in response. "This way please sir."

As Malone followed him, a faint ghost of a smile, washed over his face.

"That should shake things up" he thought. Now to see what falls down."

"The warden's office is right this way sir," simpered the guard, visibly shaking under the influence of agent Malone's dominance.

They got into a modified golf car, used for moving personnel, quickly around the facility. The golf cars, were everywhere that the inmates were not. With a penitentiary that size, housing nearly thirty thousand, of the worst possible men, that America could give birth to, you needed to be able to move your people around fast, to respond to everything and anything.

There you needed muscle and lots of it.

The two of them headed North in the cart. That's where he was, the warden. In the northern most point, of the first pentagon, looking high over the whole facility. The king of the castle.

And man, did Malone hate the wretched creature. Even the thought of that sweaty, uncouth animal, pissed him off. Even the wardens smell, offended the pristine agent Malone.

"Over there, commander," declared officer Delgado over the coms, to commander Rico.

"Team beta, come in," voxed Rico, over group coms.

"Sargent Hudson of team beta. Come in sir." came the response.

"Hold position and monitor. Team Gamma, follow us," ordered Rico, as he veered right to Delgados direction.

A small way off, something stood out in the hot desert, slightly obscured, but definitely out of place. Commander Rico with officer Delgado, pulled up a few feet from the object, no longer obscured, but clear as day.

The smell of the body in the sand, was eye watering in the intense heat.

An inmate's bloody, pulped, body, lay mangled in the sand. Dark clumps of dried blood, with black swarms of flies, feasting on the rotting body, of Rufus, the old Nazi man

Delgado crouched down to examine the scene, to gather more pieces of the puzzle. He took in the scene, gathering the clay of data, that make the bricks of deduction. Soon it would become clear to him, soon.

His eyes swept the body, then the sand. Walking around the pulp of a man looking, and then 'click', the gears of his incredible mind meshed.

"The same here as before sir, the fight caught up with them, one man, our friend here's attacker, stumbled that way, he's disoriented and dehydrated, but he's probably dead now any how's sir. The rest of them, all fifteen, headed out this way," said Delgado, indicating the opposite direction to Bubbas tracks.

"Team Gamma?" voxed Rico, into his shoulder coms.

"On it, commander, we'll find your straggler," reported in team Gamma, over the air way.

"Stay in contact, catch him, kill him and get to our position." ordered the commander, to the advancing swat van.

"Roger that sir" replied the vox communicator of team Gamma.

"Let's roll" ordered Rico, to teams Alpha and Beta.

"Delgado, take us to our prisoners." ordered commander Rico, patting the man on the shoulder.

The bikes and hummer continued the hunt with reviewed Vigor, knowing their quarry was nearby.

"Commander Rico, come in, over." crackled the coms, "Rico here, what's your situation Sargent? Demanded Rico.

"We have captured your runner sir, but he's half dead and delirious. Said he met the Devil on that bus," mocked the Sargent.

"Question him, then shoot him," ordered Rico as if it was nothing, and in the broader scheme of things, it was.

"Sir" returned the Sargent's voice once again.

"He, said he has a message, only for you. He mentioned you by name sir, I think it's important." barked the voice of Sargent Suarez.

"How did he even know my name? Trank him and blank him. Re-join us on the chase. I'll interrogate him after we get our man, over." replied commander Rico, the pitch of his voice somewhat puzzled and concerned.

"Roger sir, we have your location, over." replied the team Gamma vox.

The converted swat team, Bear cat van, kicked sand into the air at the power of the beast setting off. Once again, dancing to the drum of commander Rico, the king of the Grunts.

"You heard the man, Trank and blank the son of a bitch," ordered the Sargent.

A technician, got out of his seat abruptly and moved purposefully to a refrigerator, built in, under one of the van's console stations and pulled out a Phile of Midazolam, the powerful sedative once used to render death row inmates unconscious during the execution.

 At that dose it wouldn't knock the prisoner out, just paralysis. He could however still feel pain, and be aware of what was happening still, but he couldn't do anything about it, not even scream.

The technician spiked Bubba in the side of his neck, his hands chained behind his back. The officer rolled the big man, face down on the Bear cat floor and thrust a black sack over his head, tightening the drawstring sharply.

"Sweet dreams boy" growled the man, down the ear of the unfortunate Bubba. The limp and unmoving, Bubba, lay terrified on the hard metal floor.

The silluette of the mine shack, became stark against the blank desert back drop, as Rico's team, approached the hiding place, of the escapees being led by the inmate Hannibal.

"This is where they were running to, they'll be half dead in this heat, the sun smokes fools like this every day. How'd they got this far commander?" asked Delgado, sweating profusely.

"Can't tell you that Amigo, but I can tell you they are locked up and desperate, so stay focused all of you," commanded Rico, with a bark.

The Hummer, with team Beta, pulled up next to Ricos bike team and disembarked the large Vehicle. "What is this place?" demanded commander Rico.

"This sir, is an illegal mine of some sort, probably gold," offered Sharky, removing her helmet, a black full visor, with a shark's face painted on it.

"Probably the rendezvous, for whoever helped them in the first-place, sir," she continued.

"Delgado?" barked Rico, getting the tackers attention.

"Look for any tracks, Sophia...help him" said Rico, removing his own helmet and placing it on the scramblers handle bar.

"Team Gamma, come in, over?" asked Rico, talking into his shoulder radio.

"Come in sir," cracked the radio in response.

"What's your twenty?" asked Rico.

"Almost on your position sir," responded team Gamma, the mobile control centre.

"good" said Rico.

"It's about to get interesting over here." smirked the commander, looking at his personal guards.

"Eye sir, interesting." said Sophia, checking her weapon with a smile of anticipation, on her otherwise stern, chiselled face. Like the look of a lioness, ready to kill.

Officer Delgado squatted down again, in the desert sand, something had his attention, something odd. "What is it brother?" asked Rico, with a tone of admiration.

He rarely encountered such skill, in such a low rank. He walked over to officer Delgado's position.

"All of the inmates came here," reported Delgado, motioning to tracks, barely distinguishable in the sand.

"Three big vehicles, probably busses, were here." he said pointing to out lining tyre tracks, merged in the sand.

"More foot prints, with our friends, joined them here," he crouched moving, squatting from spot to spot.

"Some ran to the van tracks, but not all of them, some of them must be in here." he said, motioning to the mine shack with a nod.

The swat bear cat sped towards Rico's position, coming to a heavy stop, and sending sand rippling, and banking up against the huge, heavy wheels of team Gamma.

The back hatch dropped heavily to the sand, as Sargent Suarez strode down, followed by his team.

"Ok, gather in," ordered commander Rico to the full team, motioning with his arms to draw in.

"The situation is as follows, our escapees met with persons unknown, in three transporters. Some of the prisoners are in here...the rest out there, but do not know how many, or who they rendezvous with," said Rico. He turned his head to the team leaders, of Beta and Gamma.

"Hudson, Suarez," he addressed them, in a no bullshit tone.

"Eye sir," echoed the two Sargent's.

"Take Delgado and re-con the vehicles, only engage if guaranteed capture. We need some God damned answers," ordered Rico, changing his plan on the go.

"Eye sir." returned the stout sargent, itchy for action.

"Delgado?" barked Rico., breaking the agent from a day dream.

"Ci," Delgado paused, "Sir."

"I want you to coordinate on my behalf" Rico returned his attention, to the two Sargent's.

"Delgado is infallible. with his skill, we will catch our quarry, he's in charge of directions, clear?" asked Rico, dominantly.

"Eye sir, Clear," returned the Sargent, with only a hint of indignation.

"I will be paying attention to your career, with great interest," said Rico, to officer Delgado.

"Ok let's do this and remember, we need some of them alive," announced Rico to his team.

"But not all of them though sir?" purred Sharky.

"No, not all of them. You can have your fun Sharky," said commander Rico, through a smirk.

Team Beta and Gamma rushed into their transport and under the advisement of officer Delgado, sped off into the evening desert, in hot pursuit of new pray. The hunters of wayward spirits could taste it, taste the forth coming slaughter, sure they would have to obey Rico's orders and leave some alive for advanced interrogation, but officer Delgado, would not be among them, not if Sargent Suarez had anything to do with it.

San Diablo, the devils haven.

CHAPTER 5.

"Sophia! you're up." ordered Rico.

The athletic Sophia appeared next to him. She turned her head to the side, to her Commander.

"I've been working on something special for you Commander," she whispered back at him, pressing a hidden button on her left vambrace, seductively.

A small red light flashed, then the whole of Sophia's black, metallic Vambrace illuminated, exposing a screen and an array of illuminated buttons, on the flat screen of her smart armour.

She turned herself to face the Commander raising her forearm towards her chest, with her other hand, she swiped across the screen without stretched fingers.

A loud click, came from her body, as a squadron of tiny drones, freed themselves from her body armour. The drones began orbiting the killing machine, code named Agent Sophia.

Sophia pointed with her right hand, to the entrance of the old mine. The drones became illuminated, spinning faster and faster around her body, circling her out stretched arm. They moved so fast that the ten, or more drones, appeared as one solid blur, of neon blue.

 She extended her index finger at the shack and in an instant, the drones had smashed through the old wooden planks, that made up the front wall.

The drones spread out in the mine entrance, taking positions in the corners and centre space of the wooden interior. Swapping places with each other and collecting data, with an Eerie grace in their synchronicity.

All the time sending images and data, to the flat screen control unit. Able to predict Sophias thoughts by reading subtle cues on her face, pupil dilation and heart rate. By all accounts, the drones and the agent, were one.

 The drones formed one single line to conceal their number, and hummed into the gloom.

"Oh Sophia, I do like your toys," flirted the commander. His time spent with these incredible individuals, had earned him the right to say things to these women, that would cost any other man their life, but the commander was no other man to those lithe killing machines, he had earned his title and his rank in their hearts and minds.

"The entrance is clear, drones checking the shaft opening, no one yet sir. Are we clear to play?" returned Sophia playfully.

"Don't kill them all... O'Hara I'm talking to you," announced commander Rico, jokingly.

"I want heads and I want data. Catch them, kill some and tie up the rest, they'll hold nothing back from me, once you cats have had your play," said Rico, as he raised a hand into the air.

"Alpha team go go go!" roared Rico, dropping the hand to his side arm.

In a silent flash, the trio were at the shack door. Sharky and O'Hara, had semi-automatic rifles, brought up to their shoulders ready, eyes trained to the sights, breath steady and controlled. They moved in with silent ferocity, like tigers on the hunt.

Sophia pulled a broach with a large black dome from her belt and placed it on her forehead. It flashed with light, as tiny wires punctured the flesh of her forehead, and blinked open, revealing what looked like a robotic, third eye.

Small metal needles, flew out of her body armour and began a rapid orbit, around her entire body. Thousands of the deadly shards, spun with such fierce speed, that it made the air around her throb and hum.

Commander Rico finished a rolled-up cigarette and flicked it into the air. He slowly strode towards the shack, gun still in its holster, confident of his team's skill and unwavering devotion to him.

He knew there would be no danger for him, he knew that no harm could ever happen to him, not while those three, drew breath.

Team Alpha lived for each other, absolutely devoted to one another, the ultimate killing team.

The commander opened the door and strode into the shack.

"Commander, have you been smoking? Hah, you're a naughty boy" scolded code name Sharky.

"They are bad for you, sir," she continued, with a big smile, on her scarred face.

"So are you, Sharky" chuckled commander Rico.

"Sophia any signs of them?" enquired the commander, his demeanour much softer, when it was just him and his elite, but no less intense and no less sharp.

"Switching to body heat imaging, commander," replied the cold, velvet voice of agent Sophia.

A low beep came from Sophia's arm piece, and the cold grey of the surrounding area, appeared in stark contrast to the bright yellows, orange and white images of the inmates in hiding. They appeared like volcanic ghosts on Sophia's screen.

She moved a finger along part of the screen, and a red rectangle appeared, with chevrons pointing in the opposite direction. She moved her finger that way, along the rectangle and 'CLICK' 'CLICK.' The drones anchored themselves into position, in the rock face of the dark, sloping mine shaft.

The sound of the tiny metal legs penetrating the rock face, echoed through the eerie gloom of the mine. The drones, had transformed from flying mode to spider mode.

Sophia's blades still whirred around her body, they suddenly flew up and began circling overhead. She held her smart screen vambrace, up towards the commander.

"Pick one sir" she said to Rico.

"Pick a prisoner," she continued, smiling at the older warrior.

Rico studied the screen for a moment, then pointed to one of the Latino inmates, a plump, tall, young man, covered in tattoos, which stood out as scales, in his heat signature.

"That one looks tasty, show me what you got, agent," said Rico, in an inquisitive and excited tone.

Sophia looked straight at him, raising an eyebrow at the rugged commander.

"Any time commander" she said seductively, pulling her eyes from him, to the screen on her forearm.

She used her thumb and forefinger, to enlarge the screens image of the man, then circled the image of him with her finger, then tapped on his image once.

The spider drones launched into action, while Rico and Sophia observed on the screen. Rico motioned to Sharky and O'Hara, with a raised hand. They stood braced, eyes shining, sinew primed and ready, their heart beats slowed down, ready for the thrill of combat.

 The drones, sneaked closer and closer to the man, until finally, they were positioned in a circle above him. In an instant, they anchored in to the rock and fired small, barbed harpoons, attached by a Hexi carbon wire, five times thinner than a human's hair and a thousand times stronger, into the man's arms, legs and back.

With the sound of a zipper being pulled fast, the man was air born, trapped in Sophia's web.

The drones shot the other end of their Harpoons, into the rock and dropped from the shaft ceiling. Rico dropped his hands, and the agents began their deadly trade, as bespoke makers of death. They bound into the darkness, on the hunt, their thirst for the revenge of their fallen brothers, soon to be quenched.

The falling drones, illuminated and became flying spies again, whirling round the spot, drawing fire from the inmates, distracting them from what was coming.

Screams for help came from the man in the web and echoed down the shaft, as the drones flew back up the shaft, passing Sharky and O'Hara, as they sped towards Sophia. They circled her once, then reattached themselves, on to Sophia's body armour.

Commander Rico put his hand on the agent's shoulder and said playfully.

"You deserve a raise agent Sophia." Then ran down the dark shaft, with his two revolvers in his hands.

Sophia set her needles in orbit again and pursued the kill with her commander, her Rico, her secret love.

She would do anything for him, anything, but fear had always stopped her from raising it with him, she feared his rejection so intensely that it burned. The thought of not serving with him, ripped at her heart like a dragon's claw.

The irony, that a woman so strong, a woman from war, totally fearless, now so timid in her heart, from the tenderness of a good man.

O'Hara sprung like a panther in the dark. She pounced on one of the inmates from behind, twisting his neck with a loud 'snap'. Two armed men fired their weapons towards her, but in a blink of an eye, she ducked down, holding the corpse up, using the man's body as a shield.

In a single, violent burst of shear barbaric strength, she hoisted the man up, above her head and threw his body into the two shocked men. Drawing her rifle to her shoulder, as the body flew through the air. 'Pop' 'Pop', she squose off two rounds and ended the men right there Without a backwards glance, she continued her quest for blood. Three more shots came from the darkness and three men fell.

Their assassin trampled over their bodies, as she advanced into the dimly lit, gloomy, wet tunnel.

O'Hara stood motionless, looking at something on the wall.

"Sup girl?" asked Sharky "you, ok?" she asked, as she moved towards the formidable O'Hara.

Weird there's no gun shots, there were more of them down here" answered O'Hara puzzled.

"They probably ran down there," said Sharky, pointing down the tunnel.

"Yeah, but look at this," said O'Hara, switching her mag light on. It was bright, intensely bright, in that dark tunnel.

Blood was everywhere, the walls were thick with it. Agent Sharky lifted a boot, the blood was sticky and tacky under foot. Blood dripped off the boot sole and dripped back, into the puddle of gore on the shaft floor. She pressed her Vox.

"Commander, do you see this?" she asked, blankly. A loud crackle of a radio, echoed just behind her.

"What the fuck happened here?" asked Rico.

"The, the, the, Devil came Holmes, came and ripped them out, I saw it man, the fucking Devil, El Diablo" screamed the shocked and terrified man, in Sophia's web.

"Let me down eh, I can help you Holmes, get me down man," begged the inmate.

Rico nodded his head and Sophia clicked her fingers, dropping the big man with a thud.

"Ahh err ahh" he moaned.

"Juice him" said commander Rico, hurrying things along.

O'Hara grabbed the man's head, with one hand and stabbed him hard, with a loaded hypodermic needle. Injecting the man, with a cocktail of painkillers, steroids and adrenaline.

"Oh, fuck man, that good shit, what is that bitch?" asked the fool.

O'Hara grabbed the man by his balls and squoze them like a vice, then let go. The inmate gingerly got up from his knees, moaning.

"What did you see, Puta?" growled commander Rico, his Latin roots exposed through his anger.

One of his elites had been insulted and he always took that shit personally.

"Fool, you best spill that shit now," Growled the commander.

"When they started shooting, I think it woke something, something big and evil, Holmes." answered the man wincing in pain, even through such strong painkillers as those.

"A big shape moved through the shadows, like a man but much bigger, it was the colour of shadow's, big, big horns and...and those eye's man," the prisoner paused, wide eyed in terror at the cold realisation of what he saw.

"El Diablo, El Diablo came himself, from the deep place, El Diablo," he broke off again, with eye's glazed over in deep fear.

"What," shouted commander Rico, shaking the man to snap him from his trance of terror.

"What next, what happened to the others, where are they?" demanded the commander.

"It came from behind them and 'Blam', a horn through two of my bredrin," He indicated a gang tattoo on his chest, slapping it with pride. You could clearly see Lauret tattoo's, indicating him as a high-ranking member of the Mexican mafia. A colonel of the notorious and brutal cartel.

"And with giant black hand's, he torn them apart Holms, he grabbed one of the Negros by his shoulders man and just bit his head off, the whole fucking thing man, no joke, then...then" he paused, looking to the floor in shame.

"Then I looked no longer man, I closed my eyes in fear, closed them tight, I was scared Essay, and so should you be, he gonna get us man," tears rolled down his trembling face.

Rico nodded to his team, they nodded back and silently surrounded the sobbing man.

"Fucking crack head!" spat Rico to his prisoner.

"Allow me to introduce you to El Diablo," said Rico, looking up to his three elite.

"Pin him," he said reaching in his pocket, to pull out a flattened cigarette.

"You, Holms, have insulted one of us, and I can't have that, can I O'Hara?" said Rico, menacingly.

"NO Commander, you god damned can't!" snapped O'Hara, gripping the man's arms tight to his sides. His panicked face twisted in horror, shaking violently, trying to escape the clutches of women scorned, screaming into the dark, uncaring void.

"It's enough to destroy my reputation, and I can't have that, can I Sharky?" continued Rico, calm and icy.

"No commander, you certainly can't," replied Sharky sternly, her voice was like broken glass in the ear.

"People would talk, and I can't have that can I Sophia?" asked commander Rico, taking a long drag on his cigarette.

"No commander, you can't." purred the agent, pupils dilated with the anticipation of blood. Rico picked up a big rock, the size of a brick from the floor and stood in front of the man.

"Have you no information, you could trade for your life?" asked the commander.

"Who were you meeting here, who was on the busses?" demanded Rico, patting his left hand with the rock. He stopped and placed the sharp and eroded tip of the rock, against the terrified man's forehead.

"Who got away?" demanded commander Rico, pushing his face in close to the man, nose to nose.

He could smell the fear on the man's breath and he liked it.

"Them white boys, they went in the RV and the rest of us, were to wait here, Hannibal had a plan," confessed the man hurriedly, his eyes crossed, and focused on the large, sharp rock.

"What plan?" asked Rico, drawing another puff from his cigarette.

He blew the smoke in the terrified man's face, "Hannibal... Reese?"" pressed the commander.

"Ci, Ci, from the transport" chirped the inmate, slightly elated and hopeful in their belief of his testimony.

"What about the other vehicles here, we found the tracks from three vehicles, who were they?" growled Rico, pressing hard against the rock. A trickle of blood ran down the inmate's face, mixing with tears and sweat.

"Listen man, I told you there was only one RV, and the Nazi's took it, took some gun's too," panicked the prisoner.

"You found gun's here?" asked Rico, intrigued.

"Ci, guns. Everything left in a hurry, coffee and shit spilt everywhere man, guess they sprung from that thing, eh?" offered the pale, sweaty, shell of a former colonel.

Rico smiled and loosened up, dropping the rock to the ground with a thud.

"Very good. The look on your face though essay," the commander joked, chuckling.

"I'm not going to kill you," continued Rico.

The prisoner stopped shaking, for a moment.

"She is!" said Rico, pointing at Sophia.

"Make it quick, were busy," he said.

Agent Sophia smiled, as she looked at the panicking, recaptured inmate.

In a whoosh of movement, the orbiting metal shards flew at the man, piercing him in a grid of agony. Every half inch of his body, was penetrated by tiny, metal spikes.

He screamed wildly, from the intense sensation, caused by hundreds of tiny needles, piercing deep within his trembling, quivering flesh.

With the power of her mind, combined with her futuristic inventions, she had full control over the magnetic fields of small metallic objects, allowing them movement and purpose. Weaponising even a needle, and those needles became a tool of execution.

The man was lifted off the ground, screaming a silent scream, stifled by an agony beyond belief. In a blink of an eye, he was a pile of minced meat, twitching on the dusty mine floor, covering the four of them in blood and gore. They wiped the blood from their faces and stared at Sophia in disbelief.

"Sorry, I forgot about the spay zone," giggled Sophia, blushing at her error.

San Diablo, the devils haven.

CHAPTER 6.

"Suarez come in, over," said commander Rico to his shoulder communicator. A momentary pause filled the mine with static, then through the crackle of radio static, came the faint, far off voice of Sargent Suarez.

"Come in commander, Suarez here," he sounded distorted and echo hidden.

"Suarez, I can hardly hear you. What is your status? Over" asked Rico, followed by a long pause, that time though, the crackle of static was more like a high-pitched Beep. The horribly distorted voice of Sargent Suarez, was almost undistinguishable from the painfully twisted, sound of the static.

"Shit" cursed Rico, angrily, frustration evident in his voice.

"The signal can't get out that far from here, it's all the metallics in the rock commander," explained Sharky.

"We just need to send the cam footage, to the bike console and remote navigate the bike computer from here and BAM! Send it to the Bear cat! Then Suarez will know what we know. You can send a message, by talking into my body cam, sir," said Sharky, turning her head to Sophia and smiling.

"See, you're not the only smart assed bitch here," she said chuckling.

She could say it, but she would not recommend anyone else to try, at least not Infront of her.

Rico stood Infront of Sharky, addressing Sargent Suarez through her body camera.

"Engaged escaped inmates in the mine, we believe they were ambushed by forces unknown, Team Alpha and I will sweep the area, in pursuit of escapees and assailants. Teams Beta and Gamma, continue as planned, radio useless in here, sending cam footage to your position, via satellite hop, would appreciate an update, sending message now," said Rico, into Sharkys chest camera. He stood fully upright and nodded to agent Sharky.

"Agent, make it so." he ordered.

The crystal-clear voice of commander Rico, filled the earpiece of Sargent Suarez hunched over one of the communication consoles, of the forward operating base, the swat bear cat, of commander Ricos team Gamma.

Sargent Suarez, listening intently, pressed his finger into his ear, blocking off most of the background noise. He pressed that firmly, on his earpiece, it was as if trying to make it louder somehow.

The eyes of Suarez became wide, as he raised his eyebrow at the footage of the colonel's confession. As the colonel shouted "El Diablo," on the footage, the Sargent, a catholic by upbringing, kissed his index and fore finger and made the sign of the cross, by touching his forehead, then naval, then left breast, then right.

A superstition to ward off evil, or at least it used to, until there. Until he got trapped in that Hell, in that damned hot desert. A shitty deal, but national security will be national security. so, there he was a prisoner just like the filth behind those bars.

Separated only by perception, and he hated them and resented them for it, all the same. A prisoner without chains, but a prisoner none the less, a guest and a slave, to the warden's whim and will it would seem.

A smile flashed across the Sargent's face; a plan was hatching.

He stood up and turned from the console, allowing himself a moment to think. Silently he stood there in prayer, justifying his plan to his god and asking for forgiveness in advance.

Suarez hastily typed on one of the consoles flat screens. Letters began appearing illuminated, at his touch and became a low blur; as he cobbled together the reply to commander Ricos message. To confirm the message and bullshit a report on the team's progress.

He finished typing and scanned over the screen with his eyes, if anything was amiss on his message, commander Rico would suspect something and Suarez knew it.

Satisfied with the contents, Suarez pressed send on the console screen. Now time for putting it all into action, he thought.

He leaned into the front passenger.

"Hey Delgardo, Rico said he's engaged some of the inmates, we are tracking those remaining, and those aiding them in two other vehicles, just as you said, Holmes" said the Sargant to agent Degado, patting him firmly on the shoulder.

"He said we leave none alive, he has the information he needs. Team Alpha are pursuing the rest now in the mine," lied the Sargant, smiling at the unit's tracker, officer Delgado.

The skittish guard hurriedly led the tall CIA man, up some metal fire escape steps. To a second-floor, viewing balcony, manned by more armed prison guards.

Malones escort pressed the intercom button. A buzz could be faintly heard, coming from the sealed off control room, responsible for access, between the two outer holding cells.

The large and heavily spiked, electric fence buzzed, then clicked, a hidden gate to the outer block opened up. Armed men flanked either side of the walkway, watched Malone intently.One of the operating team, opened the door. A short and stern looking officer stood in the opening.

"He's expecting you and he's madder n Hell in there, hope it was worth it mister," she shouted, to special agent Malone.

 "Thank you, mam," replied Malone, as cool as a snowman's nose. Without missing a beat, he walked on.The guards on the viewing balcony, slowly closed in, weapons at the ready.

His escort, the once petrified guard, suddenly grew back his balls, and turned around smirking at the special agent.

"That's far enough, Mr fancy pants! When a man skates on the ice, he ought to" ...'Crack', agent Malone interrupted the now brave guard, by breaking his neck and taking his gun.

With the speed of a rattle snake, he cocked the shotgun and fired point blank, at the nearest guard's crotch, castrating the guard, but not killing him.

He side stepped the wounded fool, and cocked the shotgun, as fast as thunder and pressed it into another guard's crotch.

He grabbed the startled man, by the lapel.

"No more games," he roared.

"Where is the warden," continued Malone, venom dripping from his voice.

The prison officer raised a trembling arm and pointed, to a raised office building, on top of the rehabilitation block.

"Above the slaves," he stammered, revealing more than he should have and Malone could taste it, like nectar on his tongue.

"Thank you, my man. Now give me your mag key" demanded Malone, removing the guards side arm and tossing it into the prison yard.

He held the shotgun up level with his shoulder, staring for a moment at the guards.

His sunglasses took in all the data and fed it, via a tiny hidden camera in the frames, to an algorithm in Jeffries computer console. Information was fed back, to the microchips in the special agent's brain, one of the secrets of his success.

Malone, shot gun still pointed, had eye contact with the guards still held fast. The impressive agent of intelligence, slowly started backwards stepping towards the blocks guard access and a large, metal door, locked fast by powerful magnets.

He made his way to the door and swiped the magnetic key card over the lock and 'click', the door opened.

"So, it's a trap, is it?" he mused under his breath.

"Time to spring the trap," he whispered to himself, then with a dry smile, he squose the trigger of the prison issue, pump handled shot gun and disappeared behind the door.

The sun was setting in the red-hot Nevada desert. Light was escaping, as the sun retreated from that God forsaken, patch of Hell.It was getting dark and officer Delgado knew that the chase would be over, once the night triumphed over the day.

Delgado hands clasped, prayed for a miracle, and he got one. The unmistakable sound of a gun fight, less than a mile away, Delgado's head snapped up in attention.

"That way, head that way" said Delgado, recharged and fresh with optimism, to Sargent Suarez.

"Roger that, step on it, Jones, move out," ordered Suarez, to the officer in the driving seat.

"Before they kill each other," said Suarez, glaring at the back of Delgados head.

Pure hate poured from his face like daggers. He took a deep breath and slowly, very slowly, let it out.

"Good man" he said, patting Delgado on the shoulder.

"Positions! Prepare for engaging armed prisoners and agents yet unknown. Kill them all, repeat kill them all!" commanded Sargent Suarez, to his team in the cat, and over the coms to Hudson's Hummer team, as they stormed towards the fire fight.

One bullet, then two more bounced harmlessly, off the Hummer's bullet proof windscreen, into the hungry night. Sargent Hudson, grit his teeth and floored the big boy towards the crowd of evil, fighting for their lives.

The sound of gunshots was deafening in the vast plain of sand.

"Arr, ARRR," growled Sargent Hudsen through clenched teeth, gripped totally by the thirst of blood. Hungry for blood, he ploughed into the two men, firing round after round in his direction. They tried to escape but too late. Not agile enough to escape Hudsen's wrath, their bones crunched under the weight of the hummer.

The gargling sound of blood, trying to escape the throat of the doomed men, audible in the cab. Sargent Hudson smiled a soldier's smile.

"It's, go time!" he shouted back to his team, as he opened the door, of the still moving vehicle and jumped out, snatching at his side arm, the desert eagle hand cannon.

He dropped to one knee and shot three times into the fray. The remaining four agents likewise, exited the vehicle and drew their weapons, eager to join the dance themselves.

The Bear cat slid to a halt and the flash of gunfire, cast a welcome to Suarez and his team. Death had entered that night, death with a badge and a gun.

"Let the massacre begin!" shouted Sargent Suarez, pumping his team to a frenzy of spite and vengeance. He pressed the departure mechanism of the swat van, unleashing Hell into a condemned Nevada night. Blood was shed and life was extinguished, in a storm of bloody vengeance.

San Diablo, the devils haven.

CHAPTER 7.

Agent Malone caught sight of his reflection in the window, of an empty interrogation room. The agent reached into his jacket pocket and retrieved a long, metal comb.

He Moved closer to the window, to better see his hair, slightly out of place. He brought the shiny comb up to his hairline. His eyes darted instinctively, to the movement of a man, advancing in his reflection.

He spun effortlessly on his heals, to meet the assailant face on. Met with the sight of a tall, rugged guard, advancing on him with his night stick in hand.

The burly guard, swung his night stick, over his head. His huge shoulders twitched, as he brough the stick down. Agent Malone squose the sides of the comb, ejecting the metal teeth of the comb into the face and head of the now incapacitated guard, on the brink of oblivion.

His clean-shaven square jaw, dropped and quivered, as the big man stood there, dead except for his muscular system, still twitching, as his life escaped from him.

In an instant it was over and the guard fell, motionless to the ground.

Agent Malone returned his attention, back to his reflection, releasing pressure on the comb. With a smooth 'click', new teeth snapped into place and the agent went back to combing his hair.

"There, that's better," he said, adjusting his suit in the mirror like window.

Malone found himself without escort, and alone, at the entrance of a long corridor. To his left, extending the full length of the corridor, was a long window, from floor to ceiling.

Square panelled glass, overlooked the yard and segregation zones. A maze of electrical chain linked fencing, punctuated frequently by gates, manned by more of the useless, armed thugs, the San Diablo prison officers.

To the right of him, was a long, uninterrupted grey wall, behind it, the prison cells of the outer pentagon block.

It was eerily quiet, as if the jail was empty, not the normal hum of a prison this size, but the inmates in this block were extremely compliant. The inmates were rewarded for their compliance, rewarded with more privileges and better conditions and facilities. All they had to do was submit totally to the warden and his experiment programme.

The men they were, now totally in contrast to the robot-like men, that they had become.

The tall agent walked the corridor for what seemed like hours, as he followed the viewing window around every corner.

The changeless view, could creep into the mind of normal men and fester like a splinter of doubt, but agent Malone, was no normal man, and without breaking step, he pressed on down the bleak and depressing corridor, of the outer block.

"Paradise falls" the guards called it, when in earshot of the inmates, and the "professes play pen" when they were not.

The echo of Malones shoes, clicking against the well-polished grey floor, bounced off every wall, making a noise like an army of marching soldiers, filled the depressing space. The echoes became deafeningly silent, as the agent came to a sudden stop.

A door opened Infront of Malone; two huge, ugly guards strode out to meet him.

"Agent Malone? he's been expecting you," said one of the guards, a tall slender man. His hands and face were heavily tattooed, with skulls and swastikas.

"Please come this way, agent Malone" said the other man, slightly shorter than the other, but extremely muscular. His guard uniform, could barely contain his physique. His face, was in a permanent snarl and covered in ritual scars, the tribal tradition of the Crocodile people of north Africa.

The two men were in stark contrast to each other, bitter enemies by all accounts, but there they were, reformed by terror and surgical intervention. An example of the warden's power, over all his people.

A vulgar display of might, for the agent to see. A message of dominance from the warden.

"Lead the way man." Said Malone, gesturing with his hand.

"No, you first," said the slender Nazi.

"I wasn't asking, I was telling! Lead the god damn way," said Malone, sweeping his jacket open and unclipping his revolver with his thumb.

He stood there, hand on pistol, staring down the men. He knew by their faces, that they realised death when they saw him. Malone let go of the gun and straightened his black tie, he paused to stare at the men incredulously.

"Well fucking move then!" he barked.

The men looked at each other and began walking towards a large, thick oak door, at the end of a short-carpeted corridor.

The large African American guard, approached the door hesitantly, as if frightened by the room. He knocked gently three times, with a trembling hand, on the warden's office door.

Two Latino gang members, fell, lifeless in the sand, victims of Sargent Hudson's hot fury. Team Beta were strafing bullets, as they zig zagged, looking for targets and tactical positions.

Team Gamma, led by Suarez, charged the fray, assault rifles to the shoulder of each agent. Staring down the sight of their heaven senders, hunting victims for termination.

Sargent Suarez stopped for a moment, crouching at the ground Infront of the Hummer for cover. He holstered his own weapon, and picked up the AK47 of a fallen gangster. He checked the fire arm over, changed the magazine for a full one, still in the hand of the dead cartel foot soldier and reloaded the weapon.

 Leaning in on the vehicle, he took aim into the fray. He slowed his breath down, and tuning himself out, until all that existed for him was the target and the gun.

He fired two shots into the fray, before the second shot hit its mark, he had dashed back to his hiding place.

Sargent Hudson, leader of team Beta and agent Tucker, from his own team, fell dead where they stood. Unwitting victims of Suarez's betrayal.

"Collateral damage" he told himself.

He wanted out of that bullshit detail and nothing was going to stop him. He hated San Diablo, he hated Nevada and he truly hated commander Rico and his pet dog Delgado, but that night he would end it all. On that night, it would all be over, but first he had some loose ends to attend to.

His plan was brutally simplistic, for such a brutal man.
He would murder his former brothers at arms, once the
escapees and their assailants, were thinned out enough.
Only then he would begin his treacherous plan.

Officer Murrey, dropped to the floor holding his
stomach, blood oozing between his fingers, onto the
desert killing field.

Officer Delgado, ran crouching from behind the brown
Winnebago RV, guns ready and in his hands. He moved
silently across the sand, stealthily approaching the dug in
position, of the escaped Nazi inmates.

They had taken up a superior position, amongst large boulders, clustered together. Well covered, well-armed and pumped on alcohol, the brotherhood, were a dangerous target.

Delgado with eyes like a cat, stalked into position behind them.

"Buenos Naches, Bastardo" hissed officer Delgado, announcing himself and initiating the violence. He opened fire, roaring as he ran at the Neo Nazis.

Two of their numbers fell, before they even had a chance to think.

The first to react was the Alpha of the group, the large shaven headed man, yanked up and opened fire with his assault weapon, but Delgado had already moved. Advancing like a bullet, he closed the distance and, in a blink, he slapped the gun away from one man and slammed the butt, of his white handled revolver, into the head of another man.

He turned his attention back to the first man. He pushed him away hard, with a powerful front kick to the man's diaphragm. Arms straight out and to the sides, he shot both men in the forehead, then he dropped to one knee, avoiding the bullet of the skin head. He drew both guns straight in front of him, firing both pistols into the man's chest.

Delgado walked over to the gasping man on the floor. Blood splashed from the skinhead's mouth, as he tried desperately to breathe and curse.

Officer Delgado, lent over the man.

"Brown power, puta!" Said the officer, with eyes of rage.

He stood looking down his arm, past his gun and back to the man, then he turned his head away and squose the trigger, once.

Delgado, reloaded his gun and looked up for the last time.

Sargent Suarez looked up from his scopes and smiled, then leaning on the vehicle, he took aim and began picking off his comrades from his concealed position, one by one, his fellow officers fell dead under the evil eye of Suarez, the betrayer.

The few surviving gang members, scrambled or limped to an old 1937 Dodge truck, black with flames on the hood and down the fenders. The four gangsters sped away into the darkness of the desert void, chased away by the haunting laugh, of the turn coat Suarez.

Sargent Suarez breathed heavily with relief. So far, the plan was on track. The disgraced officer, walked over to one of the Latino gangsters and began undressing himself in the cold, star light.

San Diablo, the devils haven.

CHAPTER 8.

"Get in here, you, starchy son of a bitch," came a gruff voice from behind the door, angrily.

Agent Malone snapped the large bronze handle, down and sharply burst open the door and strode into the office purposefully.

"And you can leave the god damn gun with the girls," said the warden, chiding the two guards like children.

The agent immediately removed his firearm, from a holster on his side and handed it to the over muscled guard.

"And that comb, doo Hicky! Mighty cool by the way" continued the warden, smugly.

Malone reached into his inside pocket, retrieved the comb and squoze the sides, ejecting the small metal teeth into the wall next to him, then handed It to the astonished guard.

Armed men entered the room, flanking the walls as they filed in, surrounding the agent on all sides. Undeterred, agent Malone, paced towards the warden's chair, with a face like thunder.

One of the guards stepped towards the menacing agent, ready to fight.

"It's ok Bill," said the warden, holding up a hand to the guard.

Malone stopped at the desk, to pull a chair out. He hitched his trousers up at the knee and sat down, turning his head behind him slightly, to address the room.

"Leave!" he said gruffly to the guards. His tone was commanding and absolute.

"Do as our friend here asks, boys," said the warden. He heaved himself, to face a massive Caucasian guard, a huge and vicious looking man. He was not like the other men, he was clean and pristine, not at all like the zombie men, usually in the wardens employ.

"Not you Mr Black, id'e like you, to help facilitate our little meeting," said the warden smoothly.

Agent Malone, stared intently at Mr Black through his CIA sunglasses. The facial recognition software, quickly matched the man's features, piece by piece, over all the images on file, from every military, police and crime database across the developed world, then moments later, the connections were made and the puzzle finished.

" Black?" is that what you're going by now days Williams?" said the agent.

"Tell me, how was Sarajevo for you, you seemed to like it at the time," taunted the agent, staring at the warden and smiling.

"Mr Black here has a past, so what, don't we all?" he paused, "but you won't find much about me, in them their fancy glasses," continued the warden, licking the sweat from his top lip.

"Mm hmmm, salty," announced the disgusting man, tasting the excretion.

"Tell me why though, Mr Malone, with all the security I let you bring, all the sedation he had and of course the FUCKING! ELECTRIC! FENCE!" he shouted, standing and banging his stubby little fist, on his desk repeatedly and frenziedly.

He composed himself and licked his sweaty palm, then the beast smoothed his thinned, wiry, white hair down.

"How with all that, my dear agent, have I got your pet superman, loose in my facility?" enquired the sweaty warden.

Special agent Malone, removed his sunglasses and meticulously folded them 'Snap', closed. He opened his jacket and returned them, to his inside pocket and cracked a smile, laughing for an instant, before again, silence. He lifted his eyebrows and leaned in towards the man.

"You promised us progress, you told us they were fully functional, no glitches. well, I can tell you that we are disappointed in the lack of progress" whispered agent Malone over the desk, his tone was frighteningly calm. He stood up as if to leave, bluffing his hand.

"What about Rambo, he sure seems tough, why didn't you prepare us properly," asked the warden, as he scratched his chin, as if contemplating.

 "Isn't it time we started sharing with each other Malone, declassify this son of a bitch and tell me what you know about our friend. You know, me and the good senator, we were good friends. We shared many interests he and I. You tell me yours and I'll tell you mine," he said, writhing in his chair, like a mockery of seduction.

"You have our file, you know as much as me," replied agent Malone, flatly.

The warden looked over at Malone, shaking his head incredulously.

"Malone, ah! Stop taking me for a fool, you wouldn't be here if I did and your man there, would be in his cell, what are you keeping from me?" asked the warden, mopping sweat from his round, blotchy face.

"Shouldn't we go somewhere quieter for this?" said the special agent, motioning with a nod to Mr Black.

"Oh, don't mind Mr Black here, you can talk freely. Just pretend he isn't here," said the warden, shrugging off Malone's concern.

"I'm going to have to insist," retorted Malone, calmly and with bluffed authority.

"No! I'm, going to have to insist, you've insisted too much already, you know?" said the warden, this time with more anger showing than before.

"You bring your own team, you kill my men, and you treat ME!!! Like a fool," he continued, slapping his chest with both hands.

The rotund warden turned his back on the agent for a moment, looking out the window, composing himself before returning his attention back to Malone.

"Mr Black stays, Mr Black here, is my own personal body guard, I vouch for his loyalty and silence personally," said the beastly man, prodding his own chest with a short, stubby digit.

Malone was silent for a moment, considering his next move, carefully.

"We will give you a little, for a little in return," he said, adjusting his ear piece and leaning back in the chair, with his fingertips touching at the tips. Like a spider, trapped on a mirror.

"Well until last week, we knew nothing at all and then from out of nowhere, Tulsa happened." began Malone.

"What happened in Tulsa, agent Malone...exactly" pressed the warden.

"As you know, Senator Poorz, was on an election campaign across the country. His Tulsa rally was his tenth stop of the tour. He was introduced to the crowd and took to the stage; when a semi naked, white guy pounced on the stage, breaking the necks of two security guards. He then proceeded to murder the Senator and his entire secret service detail," Malone paused for a moment, brushing dust of his knee from the warden's filthy desk.

"Unarmed?" asked the warden, in an impressed impersonation.

"Yes unarmed," replied Malone, rubbing dust from his fingertips, he looked up again from his hand, back to the warden.

"You know, you really are a dirty bastard," he said with disdain.

Mr Black growled with indignation at the agent and stepped forward, only to be stopped by the warden's stubby hand, on his leg.

"Good girl, do as your told. Get back in your corner princess," mocked agent Malone, provoking the guard with a wink.

"Kujo" spat Malone, to the big man and blew him a kiss.

"Stop that immediately Malone, stop trying to distract from our little chat," said the warden, moving Mr Black back.

"How ever did you arrest him; it was you wasn't it? The arresting agent, I mean?" continued the man, obviously knowing more than he was showing.

"I think you already know that" said the agent, replacing his glasses.

"Those men of yours, the ones that got in the way... what about them?" inquired Malone, shifting the power play in the room, back to his advantage.

"What about them?" asked the warden, a look of amusement washed over his round, rat like face, and lingered for a while in mockery. Then, like so much sweat before it, slid off his face and into the room.

"They were not actually guards were they, but your mad professors' failures," smirked Malone.

"Sit back and wait for it" he thought, and he didn't have to wait long. The sweaty little man, jumped to his feet and in surprising time, for a man constructed so, was stood enraged, Infront of Malone.

"Temper, temper," mocked the agent, wagging a finger at the man.

The warden looked like he was going to explode,

"Ass hole!!!" shouted the squat man, furious.

"You're going to pay for that one Malone. Now HOW. DID. HE. COME. TO. BE. YOUR. FUCKING. PRISONER?" demanded the warden, slowly and sarcastically.

"He didn't just hand himself in to you, did he?"

"You know he did," scowled Malone, pretending to be hurt.

"Not so simple as that though, was it? What did he say to you, exactly? And no more fucking about, I'm too God damn old to be hiding three dead CIA agents, you understand? You shit spouting son of a bitch!"

threatened the warden, somehow looking quite bigger than before.

"Ok, Ok," said agent Malone through a grin.

His speciality was emotional triggers and their physiological response. He could make anyone that angry, that they became stupid and allowed the truth to slip out of their lies.

"Professor Leibstein is a brilliant man, his genius has kept this facility running, you know. When we first built this place, all I had to run it was gutless, whining, do Gooders. You can't do this, you can't do that, prisoner's rights," he continued, in a mocking, feminine tone.

"The place could not run, and our holy work was in peril, and that's when we had an Apiphany, an experimental procedure," he pushed his hand in a pocket, and pulled out half a dust covered, cheese sandwich, then sat back down, under the watchful eye of agent Malone.

"All sanctioned and signed off by your boss may I add, we erm...adjusted the guards that we had," he continued.

"Adjusted, how?" enquired Malone, leaning in to catch a glance of the paper work on the warden's desk.

"Let's just say that they, Err, received certain medical procedures." Agent Malone interrupted him again, "What sort of procedures...exactly?" pressed Malone, his face void of emotion.

He moved in closer to the warden, he hated the stench, but a point must be made, and that point is you don't frighten the CIA and you damned sure, don't want to hide anything from them.

"You know, nothing much. A few implants here, a few psychotropic drugs there, all resulting in fully functioning, full compliant slaves. At MY complete control," boasted the warden.

Without missing a beat, Malone snorted in ridicule.

"I'm not impressed, what happened to the original guards? Those goons I levelled up for you, were never guards, were they? So, what happened to the big success?" he said, mocking the warden's achievements.

"Enough now, quid pro quo, it's your turn to talk! Now what did he say to you?" demanded the warden, visibly pleased with himself, for turning the conversation back to his advantage.

Agent Malone sighed and once again placed his hands together, fingertips touching.

"I was nearby with a team making an arrest," began Malone, touching his ear piece.

"Who were you arresting?" said Mr Black for the first time, without growling. He had a deep and smooth, eastern European accent.

"I won't give you a name, but I tell you, he was a valuable target. A banker for an extremist group, operating cells, from Tulsa," said agent Malone, to the bodyguard, Mr Black.

Malone turned his face, back to the warden.

"Please go on," said the warden, dismissively leaning back in his chair.

Malone could see through the warden's pretence, he also knew that this meeting was being recorded, that's why he pierced the wall with the comb device. The second and final round of teeth, were not only microphones, but also emitted a low frequency disrupter.

Scrambling any other attempts to record a meeting, with one of the CIAs top operatives, Special agent Malone.

He could barely stop the smile from forming at the thought of the warden, playing the footage only to get white noise and static on visual.

Malone sat upright in the chair, adopting a more tense posture. It was the agents turn to pretend now in that game, by assuming an uncomfortable demeanour, as if the information was being forced from him. All according to the plan.

"I got the call from the director, to assume command of local law enforcement and to capture the assassin" offered Melone, feigning fealty.

"We arrived at the scene quickly. The place was empty, except the dead men, and... Him" said Malone, frozen as he relived the fateful day, in his memory. Mindful not to give away anything valuable.

"He was on the built-up stage, completely naked, sat cross legged in the lotus posture. There was blood everywhere, but not a drop on him! He just sat there, as if meditating, totally still. He was unarmed, so I gave the order to capture," continued special agent Malone, to a now captive audience.

"How did that work out for you?" asked Mr Black, feeling happy at the thought of the CIA man screwing up.

"I had thirty men at my command. We fanned out, surrounding him with gun barrels," said Malone, glaring at the man, from behind his mirrored sunglasses.

"I ordered him to stand down and sent five local officers, revolvers out and pointed at him, to make the arrest. He was so still, motionless...until he was touched.

 It happened so fast, I couldn't make out in the blur, exactly what had happened, but the entire team were dead," Malone paused for a moment, He clicked his neck, then pushed his sunglasses up his nose with his middle finger.

"I gave the order to shoot. The noise was incredible in that stadium, as twenty-six firearms unloaded. Most of the locals, shot each other in the crossfire. He moved with such agility and speed, that we hit nothing, but the shadows he left behind. In a blink, he disarmed the rest of us. Then it happened, he just appeared in front of me, without me even seeing him move, and he just stood there, naked, covered in ash," Malone stopped talking for a moment, adjusting his cufflinks before continuing.

 "He lent into me. I felt terrified in his presence, then he said, are you agent Malone? Before I could answer, he picked a service revolver up and pointed it straight at me. 'Yes, I am he' I confessed, then he did the strangest thing, he handed me the gun, handle first. Looked me dead in the eyes and said 'I surrender.' Special agent Malone, I am your prisoner, then he knelt on the floor with his hands behind his head," agent Malone placed his hands on his knees and lent forward a little, half a smile on his face.

"Your turn, quid pro quo" said Malone to the warden.

"Quid pro quo, nothing! What did he say to you, damn it?" roared the warden.

"No, No, No, Mr Bub; yes, we know about that...it's your turn. Quid pro quo," said special agent Malone, sarcastically. Returning to his composure, he turned back to stone.

San Diablo, the devils haven.

CHAPTER 9.

Sargent Suarez, fastened a gold chain behind his neck, the final piece of his wardrobe change. He had found a dead Latino gangsters' body, his size. He swapped clothes with the ex-gangster...now corpse, right down to his jewellery and socks.

"No, No, you're too pretty" said Suarez, pointing the loaded AK at the dead man's face. He pulled the trigger, blasting round after round into the dead man's face.

"Much better," said Suarez kissing his blood drenched fingers, like a chef achieving perfection in taste and texture.

"Now even I think you're me!" he laughed, then began whistling the old song, 'Viva Las Vegas'.

The ghoul entered the swat bear cat, returning moments later, with some of the unit's tools in a bag. He Stopped only to dance a few steps to his whistling.

He opened the driver side of the Hummer and tossed the gathered tools, onto the driver's seat and disappeared inside the big old vehicle.

Within minutes, he re-emerged holding the teams tracking and communication units, in each hand. He launched them into the burning RV, and re-entered the

Bear cat, ready to sabotage the control centre, by altering and corrupting all correspondence to Rico.

He trembled at the thought of getting even at the bastard.In a burst of rage and AK47 fire, Suarez laid waste to the old swat van from within. He stepped out of the wreckage and turned to face its bullet, riddled shell.

He held up two hand grenades to his face and flicked the safety catches off with his thumbs.

The pins pirouetted in the air, bouncing off the floor either side of his feet.

"Adios mi Amigo" he said, kissing the live grenades and tossed them, into the belly of the Bear cat.

The old swat vehicle, lifted off the ground from the sheer force of the explosion. The dark shell of the vehicle, was solid black against the intense yellow flames, from the fire within. The loose fabric, of Suarez's open shirt, fluttered in the blast from the explosion, then was still again, as Suarez stood there motionless, as if hypnotised by the dancing flames of the van, much like those waiting for him in Hell.

He shook his head and turned towards the Hummer, whistling once again. Then came the next part of his diabolical plan, he only had thirty-two hours to take care of Rico and his bitches. He knew that teams of agents, would be dispatched, after two days of no contact, but that was plenty of time for a man like that. Driven by loathing and hate, to murder his former comrades and commander.

His intension was to disappear in to the hum of Las Vegas, but his hate delayed him, he would not leave without his pound of flesh. Not now.

Sargent Suarez looked back over the carnage he had wrought. The ghosts of the fallen, had already crept into the disgraced agent's deep subconscious. Angry ghosts, of those he commanded, those who trusted him, were rising in his mind, to seek their vengeance.There would be a reckoning, and Suarez knew it.

"But not until I get that son of a bitch" he declared to his god, through the darkness of the desert void. Suarez shook himself out of his daze and turned his attention back to finding supplies for his plan.

The warden looked up at the formidable Mr Black, pulling his shirt to get the big man's attention. Reluctantly, Mr Black pulled his eyes off Malone and grunted at the agent, then dragged his eye's down to meet the warden's, stern gaze.

"Mr Black!" snapped the warden, pulling the man back to discipline.

"I want a full report on today's event's, I want your full report, as to how you intend to find, capture and contain this man... well, we shall assume he's a man... and I want a written apology, to agent Malone."

"What for? Fuck these pieces of shit," interrupted Mr Black, enraged.

The warden snatched off his hat and crumpled it in his stubby little hand and began beating Black with it.

"And I want them now!" barked the warden, at the livid Mr Black.

"Now fuck off," continued the warden, sitting back down in the rhino skin chair, dismissively.

Mr Black turned on his heals and stormed out of the warden's office, glaring at special agent Malone, every step of the way. The big man, full of rage, stopped for a moment at the door, turning back to face the room, he glared at Malone.

"Will see you around" he snarled at Malone.

"Now!!!" screamed the warden, standing up and leaning over the desk.

The warden, on his tip toes lent over the desk, dripping sweat and spit on the papers in front of him, as he reached over, for an ornate ivory and gold cigar box. He opened the lid, with a flick of his stubby, mottled thumbs, revealing the contents therein.

The bloated frame of the warden, squeaked and jiggled as he strained, grunting, as he reached in to the box, with an outstretched hand.

Malone watched on in disgust, at the sight of the warden's bloated abdomen, hanging out of his sweat stained shirt, spilling onto the desk. It sickened the special agent and if not for his incredible discipline and training, it would have shown.

The warden placed a small disc, on to the table in front of him and pressed the centre of it firmly. There was a soft, mechanical click sound, then lines appeared on the disc, then another 'click', followed by a snap. The disc transformed into a miniature satellite receiver, revolving clockwise slowly. A small light flashed, from red to green.

The warden tucked his shirt back into his trousers, with a grunt.

"So, we are not, overheard," said the warden, smoothly.

"I'm sure you understand, agent Malone. What we discus here, cannot leave this room, it is a matter of national security and must be kept, absolute secret. Do you understand, special agent Malone?" continued the warden, sterner than before...ruffled somehow.

Malone could sense the warden's discomfort.

"You have my word," said Malone smoothly.
"Whatever that's worth" snarled the warden.

"This facility has total immunity, to conduct our blessed duty without prosecution or hinderance. May I remind you, agent Malone, how far above your chain of command I actually preside," boasted the warden.

He sat back in his chair, the upholstered Rhino leather, creaked under the strain of the warden's gigantic rump.

"Any speaking about these events, I am about to share with you, will not be tolerated by ourselves or the CIA. Your testimony will be ignored and you will be tried for sedition, there upon you would be sentenced," he looked as seductively as he could, licking his lips and batting his eyes at the agent.

"Then you'll be mine," said the warden, through a maniacal chuckle, "do we understand one another?" he asked sarcastically.

"Am I supposed to be scared?" smirked Malone.

"You have my word, whatever you say here, will stay here. Now, Mr Bub, you may enlighten me" smirked the special agent.

"Don't ever call me that again, it's warden to you, agent!" roared the warden, flustered by the CIA man's forbidden knowledge.

"What happened to the guards? Not those trained chimps I've met, but the original guards, where are they?" enquired Malone, unphased by the warden's rant.

"The original guards were too soft, most of um had breakdowns in the first month. Some refused to follow orders, eventually there was only my dear little friend Mr Black left, who would do as he was told. Of course, we ah, had to modify his body somewhat, you know, make him strong and big, he was almost a foot shorter, before the doc got a hold of him," answered the warden.

"What happened to them?" continued special agent Malone, pressing the vile creature further into a psychological corner.

The warden lent forward and held his flat hand against his face, as if shielding the words from the eyes of others.

"We received the go ahead from above the white house, to begin the advanced program... on the guards. The personal staff of the good doctor, gassed them all to sleep and totally incapacitated them. Then chained and bound, the program began," explained the warden, in a mock whisper.

"Tell me about the program," pressed Malone, hungry for information.

"Times up, it's your turn to answer. Why ever send him here, why didn't you just... you know?" he put an imaginary noose over his neck and "crick" said the warden.

"It's not as simple as that, but you already know that, So, what is it you actually want?" said Malone, with a snap of indignation to his tone.

"The same as you of course! What happened when you tried to...er... settle the score, shall we say?" continued the warden, pleased with the gap he had made in Malone's psychological armour.

"I stormed into his holding cell, with ten of Tulsa's best; I needed to find out how he knew who I was, but he did not want to talk. At first, all we could get out of him was RUDRA, it was all he would say, his voice was like a punch to the head, so heavy and dangerous that it could make even your skin crawl," continued Malone, confident he wasn't giving the warden, anything he did not already know.

"He was sat there on the bed, legs crossed, eyes closed and laughing. Well, that really panicked one of the officers, who proceeded to instinctively draw his revolver, but before I could stop him, the prisoner had sprung like lightening, disarming the firearm and starting a riot. By the time I could react, I had already lost five loyal officers of the law and in a flash, I was on the floor regaining consciousness, with him stood over me, with a hand stretched out at me.

 He grabbed my hand and staired right through me," Malone smoothed his hair down with his hands, pausing for moment.

" He said, I am Rudra, that's all! The last officer fell silent on the floor, then he said in an upper-class, British accent, that he was the chastiser of miscreants, and he told me why he killed the senator, you pervert. He confessed on tape, as if he was waiting to be alone before he could talk. I asked him how he knew my name and he just went back to meditating, as if I wasn't even there. It went from bad to worse after that," continued agent Malone.

"Worse, how?" said the warden, in a pretend state of suspense.

"Your turn again now, big boy" reminded Malone, "What happened, exactly to the guards?" asked the agent.

"How did he end up here, FUCKING up my prison," roared the warden. Malone didn't react, he never reacted, and that in itself, drove the warden crazy.

The warden, red with wrath, slammed his hand on the desk, hard this time.

"Why did you bring him here?" demanded the vile warden.

"The order came from high up, way above my pay grade, how should I know?" lied Malone.

"Don't take me for a fool, it's your Hancock on the transfer papers and your name on the request, you ARE, the way higher up, you bullshitting son of a bitch! Why did you send him here?!" screamed the warden.

"Two reasons" laughed Malone, enraging the man to boiling point.

Malone smoothly stood up, pushing the chair back in place with one hand, checking his watch with the other.

"Free up some time tomorrow, I'll come for your report and an update. At exactly thirteen, thirteen hundred tomorrow," said special agent Malone, in a flat authoritarian tone.

"MALONE!" roared the warden.

"What two reasons?" he continued.

"One... He demanded to come here and in exchange, he allowed us to cuff him," revealed Malone.

The warden consumed by rage, stamped his feet in anger.

"Do you know what he is Malone, you fucking idiot? He's a fucking Aghori, now I have some...some...some fucking shadow dancing, Man God, death cult mother fucker, hiding in my fucking prison!" screamed the warden, dizzy with the realisation of it all, he sensed treachery, Hell, he wouldn't be impressed otherwise.

Malone had taken the scenic route to confirm his suspicion. An Aghori Rudra, hiding here, now, when they are close, so close, to catching the war criminal Von Leibstein. Malone felt the hand of fate, on his dutiful shoulder.

"Warden he's not hiding. He's watching." Said Malone, matter of factually, straightening his tie with an all-knowing smirk, on his featureless face.

"And two. How else would I be able to be here? Now I expect your typed, report tomorrow," he continued, turning towards the door.

"You're going nowhere, but the morgue you bastard, ...BOY'S GET IN HERE!!!" shouted the warden to the door.

San Diablo, the devils haven.

CHAPTER 10.

There was a muffled sound from behind the thick oak door, the sound of three heavy men, hitting the floor hard, followed by a knock, echoing through the room.

"Thats my ride, see you tomorrow, warden. Y'all have a good evening now, COME IN." shouted Malone, flatly. His eyes never left the warden, his gaze lingered at the discomfort of the man.

The heavy door opened into the warden's office, and two crisp looking CIA agents, stepped over three huge unconscious guards.The lifeless bodies of the guards, lay strewn across the corridor floor.

"You're late" said Malone to Jeffries stepping over the first of the men. Malone paused for a moment and turned back to the livid warden.

"Thank you for your cooperation warden, I'll be sure to thank you in my report," said Malone, coldly.

"You've made a BIIIG mistake Malone," snarled the warden, to the disappearing agents as they closed the door behind them. Silence filled the room like a shadow of doom. The warden stood glaring at the door, with wrath oozing from him, like toxins from an exhaust pipe.

"A Big fucking mistake" he snarled in a deep, primal, bestial voice, like an angry monster from folk lore.

He opened his top desk draw and after a little rummaging, pulled out a little white mouse by its tail. The mouse, kicked and wriggled in desperation, as the warden held the creature above his face. The mouse dangled terrified, above the wide-open mouth of the warden. His mouth grew bigger and bigger and his teeth became less like the rounded, use worn pegs, normally adorned by the man, but became more like fangs. Long, sharp and sadistic fangs.

He dropped the mouse in his hole and chewed hard. Blood squirted out of his vicious looking mouth and down his disgusting chin, as he chewed the poor creature. He licked from his chin to his cheeks with an enormous, purple tongue, mopping up as much blood as he could, with as little effort as possible.

"He gave you nothing and you gave him everything" said Jeffries to Malone, incredulously.

"Oh, it's what he didn't give me that's of the most value. I got more than enough," said Malone, to both the agents escorting him, through the endless corridor.

Night had set, making the echo corridor, louder somehow. The feeling of being so vulnerable, so visible in the stark darkness of the outside, would freeze most people to the spot, in anxiety, but the CIA do not employ most people, only those made of stone and of all those staunch, servants of democracy, there were none as stoic, as special agent Malone.

"Black!!!" shouted the warden, adjusting his face back into place.

"Black!" repeated the foul-mouthed warden.

The muscular Mr Black, stepped over the guard's lifeless bodies and into the warden's office. "Good meeting boss?" asked Mr Black sarcastically. Filling the door frame, with his huge presence.

The three special agents walked in perfect unison, without speaking a word. Until they arrived at the locked, metal door, at the entrance of the viewing balcony.

A litter of unconscious, bound and gagged guards, slumped against the viewing balcony wall.

"We need them to open the door," said agent Stirling, grabbing one of the men, and pulling him up under his arm to keep him upright.

He held the man's hand up to a senser pad, threading his ring finger into the identification loop. The heavy steel door clicked open and agent Malone, stepped through it first.

"De-briefing in the car. Do you have your reports ready?" asked Malone, marching past the dumb-struck guards.

Malone suddenly stopped at the entrance gate, a nervous prison officer ran over to them, waving a mag card.

"Thats alright officer, I'll use mine," said Jeffries, pulling out his CIA, ID card.

He touched it on the pad on the wall, and 'Beep', the gate opened. Without even looking back, the three agents stepped out of the unit like they owned the place. The gate slammed with a bang, behind them.

"Well?" enquired agent Stirling.

"Oh yes, no mistake about it," answered Malone.

"So, as you suspected, HE'S our other man," contributed Jeffries.

"And you've just pissed him off," said Sterling, smirking slightly.

"No. I've made a relationship with him. Now he will want to talk to me. Now he will make time for me, and soon, we can get this shit hole closed," said Malone to the others.

 "And the inmates?" asked Jeffries.

"Fuck em, they are officially dead anyway," said agent Stirling, with a shrug.

"And the Rudra?" asked Malone.

"Oh, he's crucial to my plan. If he is, that is, what fat boy thinks he is." said Jeffries, opening the car door for Malone.

 The three men got in the long, black car and drove off quietly, illuminating the gloom with the head lamps, like a spectre haunting the intake yard. They drove through the many checkpoints, lighting up the sand and dust, until they finally came to a stop, at the lush, green part of the complex.

The visitor facility was like a different world, compared to the rest of the prison complex. Its green gardens stood out, like an oasis in the bleakness of the hot desert dust bowl, they call San Diablo.

The long, sleek car, came to a smooth stop outside of the quarters, allocated to the three staunch, special agents.

Agent Stirling switched the cars headlamps off, covering the area in pure darkness, once again, around the agent's unused home.

Agent Jeffries pulled out a small disk from within the glove box, similar to the device used by the warden, to scramble any method of eavesdropping. Enabling the special agents, to speak freely.

"How many did you get to talk to?" Malone asked Stirling.

"Only two, until they were fetched out by my escorts," reported the gruff agent.

" From the good behaviour unit?" Malone asked the agent, not looking up from the considerable dossier, compiled by Jeffries.

"Yes, special agent Malone, the 'Louis DeCyphr' unit"

"The Louis DeCyphr unit?" said Malone, his head up, paying more attention to Stirling than the dossier.

"How very interesting" continued Malone, pausing a moment in thought, before snorting in amusement and disdain.

"How sedated did they appear?" said Malone, returning his attention, back to the documents in his hand.

"Fully brain scrubbed, it was like talking to a smiling robot. They didn't blink, they just sat there, bolt up straight, hands flat on the table, and eyes wide open with a big stupid grin, creepy sir," reported Stirling.

"What dosage do they dope them Jeffries?" asked Stirling, turning his face at the neck, looking emotionless and flat at the profile of Jeffries, fervently cross referencing, the plethora of screens at his fingertips.

"They don't dope them in that unit," said Jeffries, closing one screen with a pinch of his fingers and opening another, with the press of a finger. Agent Stirling, tilted his head inquisitively, at an angle.

"It's all done with surgical intervention, the whole procedure is completely locked down "said Jeffries, answering the silent, follow up question from agent Stirling.

Malone lifted his head, about to issue an order.

"On it, sir," answered Jeffries, closing multiple screens.

"But it will take some time," continued special agent Jeffries.

Malone and his team could anticipate, one another totally, they were not three individuals, but a complete, single entity.

Functioning as one, they stalked the truth through the night, searching through endless prison records, prison blueprints, absolutely anything that could aid them in catching, if they could, the Rudra and anything, absolutely anything, about the top-secret experiments, carried out on those desperate for privileges, for a more comfortable time.

Those who would agree to such a thing, and it was amazing what these desperate, dead men would agree to, for even the shadow of a hope, in that desperate corner of hell. Abandoned by hope, in those dark days.

The black hummer moved through the dark desert, like the ghost of midnight. Moaning and rattling, the tortured vehicle came to a sudden stop, in the cold desert sand.

Steam, hissed violently and plumes of thick black smoke, billowed out from the engine, only to vanish instantly into the cold void, of the dry Nevada night.

"No! No! No! No! No!" pleaded the treacherous Sargent Suarez.

"Shit, shit, shitty, shit, shit," yelped the disgraced Sargent, Panick gripped, alone in the desert.

He had to think fast, he needed to act. He took deep calming breaths, allowing his training to take over. He snapped out of the grip of Panick and into the mode of action.

Sargent Suarez grabbed a green, canvas duffle bag from behind and quickly, but smoothly, filled the bag with what weapons and ammunition, he could put his hands on. Quickly, grabbing water and a first aid bag, he pushed open the roof, trap door. Giving him access to the backup vehicle.

Anchored to the Hummer roof, was the Hayes M1030 desert motor cycle, equipped with two rockets and a forward-facing machine gun. Suarez set to task untethering the desert shark.

He stood the bike upright, above the flaming Hummer and climbed up, on to the beast.He fired the motorcycle up and scrambled off the Hummer, off the bikes back wheel and sped off, into the night. The bike roared like an angry Lion, as it ripped across the desert sand.

"Computer, launch voice command," shouted Sargent Suarez, to the on-board console AI, of the powerful desert shark.

The space in front of him lit up, as the holographic face of a young boy, illuminated in his visor.

"Computer, find the last location of team Alpha," barked Suarez, to the child faced hologram.

A map appeared in the space in front, showing the way to Rico's last position, as a crooked line, pointing to a pulsating, collection of dots. The mind of Sargent Suarez, swam with possible causes of the vehicles malfunction.

"Maybe I hit a rock or something, or, yes, yes it was a stray bullet, yes, that's it," he tried to tell himself, but he knew, deep in his heart, what caused the Hummer to breakdown. He suspected it anyway.

That thought gnawed at his mind like a worm, driving him mad. That karmic retribution, had already began.

He feared the wrath of the dead, far more than the fear of death. He knew he must abandon, that foolish mission of destruction, before it could consume him totally, but he could not stop now.

He had become obsessed by the idea of killing the commander, ever since Rico embarrassed him, on their last mission.

Rico had slapped him down, Infront of his own team, for slapping agent Sophia on the ass. Oh, and was Suarez ever obsessed with her, he would have her, at all cost.

Propelled by lust, fear and hate, Sargent Suarez sped through the desert, spitting sand and anger, behind him in the night. Full throttle, he raced to his fate.

The line on the indicator screen became smaller and smaller, as the wretched Sargent drew nearer and nearer, to the pulsing dots on this visor.

His heart thrashed with adrenaline; indeed, he was drunk on it.

Commander Rico, reloaded his weapon and checked over his personal equipment. He removed his shoulder radio, leaving it in a neat pile on the dirty shaft floor.

"Sophia, I need your spies to scout, for survivors and re-con for our arrival. We need to uncover why they

rendezvoused here. What else is hiding down there?"
said Rico quietly

"Let's find out" said commander Rico, smiling at his
elite team Alpha.

Sophia pressed her vambrace, and once again, her body
armour clicked with the sound of drones unlocking from
her. The air hummed with the low noise from the drones
hovering, then a Whoosh, they flew down the dimly lit
mine shaft, off into the gloom.

Sophias vambrace lit up, as the feedback data from the
drones, overlapped on the screen. They became one,
crystal clear image of the mine interior.

A large room opened up, after the initial mine shaft and
the drones began filling into their new surroundings,
with a mechanical, but beautiful, synchronicity.

"That's, that question answered, commander, the mine is
a cover for a meth lab," snarled O'Hara, illuminated blue
from Sophias imager vambrace.

"Anchor them Sophia, and set your monitor to record
images. We will have to document this for Malone,"
ordered commander Rico, to his team.

"Consider it so commander," answered Sophia, swiping
down the screen with the palm of her hand.

The indicator lights on the drones, flickered from blue to green, as the drone propellors transformed into the sharp, insect like spikes, of 'spider 'mode', switched on by agent Sophias silent command.

Smooth mechanical 'clicks', quietly echoed around the large room, as the spider legs anchored the drones, into tactical positions around the chamber. To record the search of the room and to act as over watch, for commander Rico and his team.

"Clear commander" declared Sophia, itchy for action.

"We do not know what may be hiding out there, or what happened to the others. Only the testimony of Mr Mince here" said Rico, brushing a chunk of flesh from his shoulder.

"Surely you don't believe that shit commander?" said agent Sharky, in a flat tone of voice.

Rico looked back at his team.

"We don't know what we could face down there. Remember who our quarry is," whispered Rico, back to his team. His voice became deeper and sterner.

"Stay frosty! Move out!" Ordered Rico, readying his weapon.

San Diablo, the devils haven.

CHAPTER 11.

Team Alpha moved into the large room and quickly
activated their respirators. The over powering smell of

chemical solvents, hung thick in the air and stung the eyes of even the stoic commander Rico.

O'Hara set off her strip light torch, illuminating the room, like a million candles.

Before them was a large room, cut out of the bedrock. Flanked across two sides lay long work benches, littered with glass chemistry flasks, gas burners, and various paraphernalia, in both the production of and use of crystal meth.

A large square table, dominated the centre of the nefarious chamber.

Commander Rico walked purposefully towards the table, shining a torch of his own. He scanned the debris, strewn along the table, and piles upon piles, of raw narcotic in the middle, surrounded by containers, and bags. Some empty and others filled and sealed, or part way to being filled, with the illicit thief of life.

"Quite an operation going on here. 'Sharky', I need you to find any big timers on the escapee list," ordered Rico.

 The lithe and imposing shadow, of agent Sharky, dropped her side pouch onto one of the workstations lining the walls, and removed a palm held computer database. The agent had already downloaded the prison files of the men and now began rapidly, cross referencing the data, for history or affiliation to large quantity drug trafficking.

The screen lit her up, casting a menacing silhouette on the lab wall.

"Sophia, re-con that passage, O'Hara, document every inch, with body cam commentary," ordered Rico, to the room.

Team Alpha smoothly and without hesitation, saluted the commander and began fulfilling his orders.

Sharky paused for a moment, her lips moving silently as she read the data on her data slate. Absorbing all the information, from the prisoner profile. She stood up straight, from her hunched posture over the meth lab table.

"Found one commander," agent Sharky announced to Rico.

He strode across the lab floor, towards the incredible agent Sharky.

"What do we have agent?" asked Rico, now standing next to her, eyes fixed on the data slate.

"Our friend back there, sir, he's our big fish, commander. His record states here," said Sharky, pointing to the prisoner transfer file.

"Hernandez Fojencio Fornandez, A, K, A, colonel El Hassay, is a top-level Colonel, of the Mariachi, drug cartel.

He was caught with three tonnes of cocaine, stashed inside the coffins, of late service personnel returning from Damaskus.

He personally murdered twenty D, E, A, agents, his cartel broke him out of the courtroom, taking the judge hostage.

he was wounded in the air strike, carried out on his mansion stronghold in Columbia, where he was subsequently arrested and sentenced to life, in San Quentin.

A month later he ordered an attack on a warden and got sent to solitary confinement, where he officially killed himself, a month later and unofficially was sent to San Diablo, with the rest of the worst. Do you suspect the Mariachi cartel, busted our target out?" asked Sharky, reporting to the commander.

"I don't know, but whatever happened here, happened either with our guy, or without him, but I do know we will follow Malones orders until we have him, or his remains." said Rico, without looking up.

"Good work agent" continued the commander, putting his hand firmly, but gently on the agent's shoulder.

"Commander, I think you need to see this," said agent O'Hara, holding a torch light, to the wall in the drug lab.

O'Hara's light had exposed; some ancient symbols carved into the rock face. A warning, left behind several millennia ago, by ancient people, long gone and too long, forgotten.

"Are you getting this sir?" asked O'Hara, her voice sounded distant, as if transfixed by a spell.

"O'Hara, are you ok?" asked Rico, a little concern in his voice.

"Commander look," she said, pointing at a relief carved into the rock, of an enormous creature, swollen with gluttony, and devouring scores of people. In its hands were humans, dripping with blood.

"Sir that looks like the warden," insisted the stoic agent O'Hara.

Commander Rico nodded in response; the similarities were uncanny. The ancient relief was surrounded by hieroglyphs, in the style of the South American tribes of old.

"Sir, these look like Mayan hieroglyphs, but that's impossible, isn't it?" asked the powerful agent.

"I'm starting to think, that nothing is impossible, in this forgotten hell hole. And it's no coincidence, that he built that god damned prison here," said Rico, transfixed on the stone carving.

"Document these separately. Just between us four, until we find out more. Sophia, how are we looking?" asked the commander, turning his attention once again, to the beautiful agent Sophia.

Sargent Suarez, arrived at the splintered remains of the mine shack door, a much different man from when he last saw Rico, at that very spot.

The desert sharks' lamp, illuminated the dusty, dilapidated, old wooden structure.Suarez laughed wildly and dismounted his ride, carelessly leaving it sideways, in the sand.

"Time to get him, get him, get her, oh, yeah! Oh, ha ha hahahahaaaa" he roared, laughing madly to the darkness. He switched off the safety, of his AK47 assault rifle and ran cackling, towards the old dusty shack.

Suarez, overburdened with the tools of murder, swung open the splintered, old wooden door and lurched inside, both rifles in hand, loaded and pointed into the middle space of the room.

His eyes tried desperately to focus, but the dim light from the lamps, high overhead, seemed to blind him. As if the low light could somehow, pierce into his own darkness, revealing, the darkness of his soul.

"You betrayed us... leave now" whispered a voice, to the once great man.

"We will make you pay" added another voice like ice, sending a judder, down his wretched spine.

As Suarez stumbled through the dim light, tears ran down his cheeks, carving trenches through the thick dust, caked to his exhausted skin.

"Leave now," whispered the voice, like menace carried on the breeze.

Suarez instinctively made his way, through the darkness of the old shack, towards the entrance to the mine.

"They know what you did, DECIEVER, they know"
whispered the voice of Sargent Hudson, from deep
within the darkness of the mine.

The crazed Sargent Suarez, snarled and span on the spot,
looking for him, but of course, nothing. The guilt
gripped Sargent, dropped to his knees in tears, insane
and exhausted in the darkness. The disgraced law man,
took a few deep, but dusty breaths, trying desperately to
compose himself, in the cold dark of the abandoned
mine.

The Sargent's mind had snapped, and the guilt,
exhaustion and utter hate, had taken its toll on the
already splintered mind, of the former Sargent at arms.

 He sobbed, just for a moment, it felt good to release the
build-up, and he loathed himself for that.

 Torn and tortured by his own hand, Sargent Suarez
angrily and with a face screwed in rage, got back to his
weary feet.

 "R E E E C C C O!" he snarled, through clenched,
bleeding teeth.

Agent Sharky moved silently, through the barely lit meth lab, to the side of O'Hara.

"Hey girl" whispered Sharky to O'Hara, photographing the elaborate and ancient carvings.

"This is really messed up. Check this out," said O'Hara, motioning for Sharky to follow her.

O'Hara stopped half way along the room. Shining her torch, she illuminated a region of the carved-out lab wall.

Surrounded by strange sigils, carved deep into the rock, three pentagons within each other. Carved into the middle pentagon, was the image of two large men, with long horns, dressed in elaborately ceremonial clothes.

One holding a captive by his arms and the other removing the captive's heart, with a long, snake like knife. Above the captive, bearing down on him, was a dragon, ready to devour the man's soul.

"Oh, this is really fucked up," sighed Sharky.

"What if he was telling the truth, ya know, about," she lowered her tone and moved closer to O'Hara.

"El Diablo?" continued Sharky. A little flustered.

She put her head on the muscular shoulder, of agent O'Hara.

Agent O'Hara, put her large, muscular arms around Sharky, placing her into a protective embrace.

Sharky had fled her native country, only ten years ago. She had met the devil in that god damned diamond mine. She had to toil in the filth, to feed her elderly father. Her mother and two brothers, were accused of witchcraft and were chopped to pieces Infront of her, by brutal men with machetes. She harboured a deep fear of the occult and a burning hatred for brutal and vicious men.

Sharky was visibly shaken with emotion, not weakness, not frailty, but raw, powerful emotion! That tiger of a woman, was charged with the stuff.

Sharky hugged her back, and the two agents stood in an embrace, for only a moment, then stood, just looking deeply into each other's eyes. The dark of the room meant nothing, to the eyes of those two souls, sharing their first second, in a new and different existence.

"I will protect you, Queen," said O'Hara sternly. Her fight instinct, spiked high with emotion.

"Ha, we will protect each other, queen," whispered Sharky, trembling with intensity.

"Sir, the shaft goes on for at least a mile, then it forks off in two directions," said agent Sophia, her elegant fierce features, illuminated eerily by the screen on her vambrace.

"Oh, O'Hara, have you documented the room?" said the commander, pulling himself from an almost trance like state.

The stone hieroglyphs, had locked him in.

"Almost commander, I'm checking the last bench now," said O'Hara, returning to her duty, blushing. Commander Rico, smiled to himself in the darkness.

Agent O'Hara, fervently documented everything on the long bench, she had photographed, every piece of equipment, every flask, everything.

"What about all this money, shall I count it?" O'Hara asked sarcastically.

"If you want, or keep what you can carry," said Rico, patting his pockets for a cigarette.

"Damn "he said, coming empty handed, from a quick search in his pocket.

The four of them stuffed as many bundles of bank notes, as they could fit in their pockets and packs

The perks of being close to the commander were myriad, but so were the demands. These agents had earned a king's ransom, in the eyes of their commander, not the pittance that they actually got paid.

Compared to the service they had given their country, this splash of cream, was nothing.

Team Alpha began the descent, of the long mine passage, under the attentive over watch, of agent Sophias spider drones. If so, much as a rat moved, she would know about it and deal with it.

San Diablo, the devils haven.

CHAPTER 12.

Disoriented by emotion, Sargent Suarez pulled a foot long plastic tube, from his webbing and shook it violently for a few seconds, then with a sharp 'snap', he cracked the tube, activating a bright red glow stick.

Haunted by the ghosts of his former comrades, he had begun to fear the darkness.

Suarez pulled a small roll, of black tape from his webbing and taped the glowing stick, to one of the AK47 assault rifles shaking in his hand. He picked the other gun up from the floor and lifted his chin. The tension in his neck released with a satisfying 'click'.

"Enough of this Puta, shaking man. Let's get him," echoed his own grisly voice, in the ghostly lit entrance to the shaft. He laughed manically and stepped into the unknown.

"Mr Black, you had better have something for me?" snapped the Warden, to the mountain of a man entering the room.

"Sir he's in the morgue," reported Mr Black, blankly.

"Good I'll let Malone know he can leave," smirked the warden.

"Why?" asked Mr Black, looking puzzled.

"Because his Aghori superman, is dead of course," laughed the warden, incredulously.

"He is not dead though, he was detected by security footage, after the slaves failed to report in," continued Black.

"Sshhh" spat the warden, tapping his ear.

"When the guards failed to report in, I ordered the section be locked down and the footage be played," said Mr Black rushing his words, with his hands out in front of him, in a token of appeasement; to try and calm the pile of filth, before he could explode.

The warden stomped over to Black and stared up, into the far-off eyes of Mr Black.

"What... the... fuck... happened, MR FUCKING, BLACK! Horse shit for brains... what was on the security footage?" rambled the warden, switching from calm and menacing, to wild and dangerous, then back again.

"See for yourself... sir" said Mr Black through clenched teeth. His jaw muscles flexed in rage and rippled like a rattle snake, hunting on the hot sand.

"Like I said, he's in the morgue, warden" said Black, handing the warden a data slate of the footage.

The warden snatched the data slate, from the big man's hand without breaking eye contact.

"And Malone?" demanded the warden, his fat narrowed eyes flashed yellow, in the depth of his face.

"Nothing. He's a high-level, CIA ghost. Service records, personnel files, absolutely everything about him, is protected data at the highest level." said Black, staring back blankly, into the vile face of the evil creature in front of him.

"You really that stupid? I want results, or your nuts in a jar! Get the fuck out of here! Go!" demanded the warden, red with wrath.

"Any news on our escapees?" snapped the warden, with a voice like vomit, stopping Black in his sizeable tracks.

"No contact from the secret service, since 16.00 hours. Last report states, team Alpha are on flush out in the desert. Team Beta and Gamma, in pursuit of persons unknown, probably the same spic cartel who facilitated the escape," mumbled Black.

"And Rico?" asked the warden, a tiny eyebrow raised in query.

"Complete radio silence sir," responded Black, flatly.

"Black, show me what I'm supposed to be looking at here," said the warden, holding the data slate clumsily, in his greasy fingers.

Mr Black lent over the sitting warden and pressed the play icon, flashing on the data slate screen.

"Don't try my patience Mr Black," snapped the red, podgy faced warden, sensing hidden smugness in the big man.

The two men's faces were glowing, as they leaned closer to the slate, playing the security footage from the prison morgue.

The corridor of the maintenance entrance, appeared on the slate screen. One second of blank footage and then, pop, he just appeared, mid step from nowhere, like an apparition.

The pranic energy of the Rudra, obscured the view of him, as if a powerful light was shining on him, hiding him from the darkness.

He took a few steps and stopped, exactly beneath the hidden security camera. His head tilted all the way back, his face, flat under the spot, facing straight at the camera.

His eyes stark and black against the light, burned with the intensity of fire, straight through the screen and into the soul, or whatever the warden had for a soul.

He stood there perfectly still, then laughed deeply and waved at the hidden camera.

The warden looked up, from the bright screen of the data slate, and looked to the enormous frame of Mr Black, who gestured to the little man, to keep watching the footage, with urgency lining his enormous, broad visage.

The Rudra began to dance wildly in the corridor, as arms and legs filled the narrow hallway, as pose, flashed into pose, moving faster and faster until he appeared everywhere at the same time.

His energy became more and more intense. Light and effulgence, turned the data slate screen totally white, as the Rudra danced his Tandev, then suddenly he stopped. Motionless on one leg, the other raised at ninety degrees and pulled inwards, his arms were outstretched from his sides and his face, turned straight to the place of the hidden camera. For what seemed an age, he remained like that, then, without warning, he vanished in a blur. Only to appear on the next screen.

The Rudra moved like lightening through the mortuary complex, until he finally ended up in the big chill.

The refrigeration unit, was a large square room in the basement of the complex. Tall walls, lined on every side, by row after row, of large drawers. Each containing the preserved body, of a fallen man.

The Rudra yanked each coffin, out from its drawer on to the centre space of the room. He began flipping the lids off the preservation units, revealing those stored within.

Horribly mutated human forms, some had horns growing from shoulders and arms, faces were swollen and misshaped.

Contorted monstrosities each of them and big ones too, all were huge, muscular and bestial looking abominations. Some wore the uniform of a guard and some, the rags of an inmate, but all had numbers tattooed on their left wrist. Identification markings of experimental programs, funded by the secret agencies of the world, ran by the devil's own emissary on earth, the warden. El Diablo, himself.

The warden watched on open mouthed, astonished, as the Rudra went from corpse, to corpse, putting his hands on their eyes and dissolving their sins, by his grace. Allowing the wayward spirit, the opportunity to be reborn, without the additional Karmic debt they had incurred, during that life. He did this selflessly, for the sake of the future world.

He punished the wicked to save them, he absorbed their filth, with his purity. For the soul's own sake, he gave them a chance at rebirth and redemption.

This is the Aghori's work. Abandoning any thought of reward, or punishment, he does what he must, that is their way.

The Aghori on the data slate, sat on the cold stone floor of the San Diablo mortuary, naked with one hand held up in front of him, palm flat and still.

He sat there motionless, until ten armed men in the black uniform, of the warden's elite guard, stormed the room.

Bullets zipped toward the Rudra, but no bullet can move like an Aghori. Dodging the deadly rounds by contorting his body, he played with death, in that cold place. He rolled to his side, and the sparks of bullets, cratering concrete, followed behind him along the floor.

He leapt forward fifteen yards, landing on his hands, then he tucked his feet between his hands. The momentum launched him, feet first into one of the assailant's faces, which he sprung off, sending the man to the ground with a sickening 'Crunch'.

The Rudra landed on another guard and wrapped his legs around the man's waist. He grabbed the guards assault rifle and lent backwards, fully using the guard's own weight as a counterbalance, then fired round, after round, into the remaining guards.

As if made entirely of rubber, he stretched his hands to the floor, doubling over. The Aghori straightened up, smashing the remaining guard under the chin with the back of his head.

The guard never knew what happened. In a flash, the Aghori grabbed the man's scalp and chin. And with a snap of violence, he put the man's chin where his scalp once was and his neck broken.

The naked man walked towards the hidden camera, purposefully.

"They belong to me now!" He said in a voice like thunder.

He grabbed the first guard by the throat and moved his mouth, close to the guard's chest. Absorbing the remaining life energy, from the fallen member of the violent elite.

With terrifying efficiency, the Rudra moved from guard to guard, each one became a dried husk, after he had taken his toll, the price for disturbing an Aghori. Swift and brutal, retribution.

"Send three units, bring me his fucking head," ordered the warden to Mr Black.

"And do not speak a word of this to Malone, Clear!" continued the flustered warden, not believing what he had seen.

He was enraged by the audacity of the Rudra, and totally in awe of his ability. He had to have him; he was the anomaly that could fuck up everything that they had worked towards, all those years.

He hung his head and sighed heavily.

"THATS ALL MR BLACK" grumbled the Warden, to the retreating frame of Mr Black, already out of the office door.

The Warden pressed firmly on a brass button, sunk into a recess under the thick Mahogony, desk top. A large flat screen, slid up from a hidden channel at the rear of the desk.

Many small frames, blinked into existence. The security and body camera footage in each one.

He tapped on the frame, for Blacks body cam and the security cameras facing out from the complex and those within the complex. The frames became bigger, dividing the screen in to five equal frames.

He stretched at the frame titled 'Black Cam', making the image bigger, as it overlapped the others. He positioned Mr Blacks body camera, mounted on the big man's chest, to the centre of the large monitor. The sweaty frame of the warden, lent in close to the imager, his mouth wet with anticipation.

Out of sheer excitement, he began to rub his crotch through his tatty, stained and horribly tight, cream linen trousers.

San Diablo, the devils haven.

CHAPTER 13.

"What about the search team?" asked Stirling, his eyes wide behind his sunglasses with realisation.

With all the excitement from the Sea knight crash, they had forgotten about Rico.

"I sent commander Rico an update myself, Rico's team are at a hide out, on search and destroy orders. Suarez and Hudson, are in pursuit of multiple gang bangers, they believe assisted in the escape," said Malone, pinching the bridge of his nose, and lifting his sunglasses from his face.

The agents rarely removed their glasses, those things relay information, wirelessly into the mind of the agent. The wearer, is able to see in pure darkness, and anticipate an attack with far more efficiency, than without them.

The agent paired to the glasses, can see what the spy wear can see, even while separated and even over a mile away. Not all agents could earn such hardware, only the very top-level agents were issued with them, only the most valuable assets were equipped so.

That's why the Warden hated Malone. He knew that top brass could get messy and he really did not need mess in his facility, not now.

"But we know Rudra is here, why don't you recall them, it's a law enforcement issue now sir" said Stirling, pausing at his holoscreen.

"Sometimes you have to unleash the attack dog, to flush out the rats. Somethings really not right here. Let Rico have his fun and I'll bet you a dollar to a dose of clap, that he finds something", said agent Malone, sitting back in his seat, smiling into the darkness.

The experienced special agent, meditated on his options, while Stirling and Jeffries, continued their research in silence.

Mr Blacks team moved swiftly and cautiously, towards the main entrance and fanned out. Each guard fully armed and in full body armour and each guard on over watch with the guard either side of him.

The warden watched on eagerly. His sweaty jowls illuminated, as he moved closer to his monitor, drool stringing from his trembling mouth.

"Hold position team Black," the Warden ordered through the vox.

"Hold" ordered Black to his team, raising his closed fist to his shoulder, indicating to his team to hold their position, but with high alert.

Waiting for the others to get into position, the Wardens eyes flit across the screen. He enlarged a frame on his screen labelled 'Hammer', for the footage of two squads of guards, emerging from the inside corridor of the main prison.

They entered the main corridor, that joined the inside of the jail, to the morgue. Taking up tactical positions, as they moved stealthily, towards the last home of San Diablos dead men.

"Team Black, move in," coordinated the warden, his excitement, barely concealed in his voice.

Mr Black gave the hand gesture, for his squad to enter the building and with mechanical precision, the door was opened and all eleven members of the squad, filed into the service corridor.

Red dots filled the narrow space, from the laser sight mounted to weapons, indicating the path of sight of each agent.

"All teams move in, execute pincer strategy and mow that son of a bitch down, where he stands!" ordered the warden, writhing in his chair. He loved the build-up to violence, the heavy silence, built more and more tension, the long anticipation of conflict, followed by the climax of bloodshed and death.

The warden's breath became so heavy, that it Began to fog the screen. The loathsome bastard, was getting off on it.

He enlarged the frame, labelled the fridge, and tapped it twice, with a trembling, stubby digit. The screen was filled, with only one frame.

The scene of the Rudra, surrounded by the open coffins, of the men altered, by the evil experiments imposed on them.

The warden looked on as the black clad guards, began to appear in both entrances to the room.

"Cloak and dagger" ordered the warden, in a peak of ecstasy.

Mr Black dropped his hands, signalling the advance. The Rudra sat naked, with his back to the approaching, would be silent assassins, as if unaware of the treachery and danger.

"Good" thought Black, stealthily moving into position.

Smoke grenades, were sent in first.

"Spark em," growled, the menacing Mr Black, to one of the guards.

One of the identical guards, threw a shock charge into the dense smoke, engulfing the silent Rudra.

Sparks crackled and licked, around the thick cloud of smoke. The light show, of twenty-four thousand volts, danced across the background, of the San Diablo cold room.

"Go! Go! Go !!!" shouted Mr Black, coordinating the loud bangs and blinding white flashes, of intense light, as flash bombs detonated within the cloud, launched in an attempt to confuse and disorientate, the meditating Aghori.

The echo of gunfire, danced off the hard stone wall' amplifying the deafening roar, of hundreds of rounds of machine gun fire; unleashed at once, into the thick cloud of electrified smoke, blasting holes in the far wall, of the morgue, adding masonry dust, to that murderous, scene of vengeance.

Many of their comrades had been killed, either by him, or because of him. Then was their moment of retribution.

The sound of hate was tumultuous, but brief. Followed by a temporary, Icey cold silence.

Mr Black gave the order to cease fire, and the final gunshot rang in the air for a moment, and then all was silent, like the lull before the storm.

The guards cautiously and very slowly, advanced towards the cloud.

Slowly, very slowly, a shadowy figure began to emerge from the dissipating fog of smoke. The guards hurriedly reloaded their weapons, mouths open in astonishment.

"GET HIM, SHOOT!!!" commanded Mr Black, pointing through the smoke.

 The wardens own head guard, was the first to open fire. Bullet after bullet, exploded through the shadowy figure in the smoke, until eventually, it succumbed to its wounds, limp and heavy on the stone morgue floor.

"Unit Delta... move in, bag and tag," said the big boss of the elite.

The merriment of the murderous guards, was brief, as two more forms, much bigger than the last, slowly emerged from the setting smoke.

"Open fire!" yelled Black, bringing his weapon back to the warm cradle of his shoulder.

Within seconds, the two figures were riddled with holes and motionless on the floor.

The smoke faded to barely a mist, and yet more figures became visible. Huge, misshaped and monstrously mutated creatures, moved slowly from the fading gloom, towards the startled warriors around the room.

The dead had risen from their cold slumber, at the wish of the Rudra. He had absorbed the pranic life energy from the guards he claimed, and directed it through himself, and into the euthanised experiments. Reanimating the cadavers, to serve his will to kill.

The monsters made a quick advance, to the position of the terrified guards.

One mutation, drove the large horn on his head into one man's chest, grabbing him and pulling him closer. Forcing the horn, straight through him, wearing him as a hat; until he himself, was cut down in a fury of gunfire, as other hideous mutations, staggered into action.

Biting, clawing and impaling as many guards as possible, before the body became a useless pile of mince, on the cold stone.

"Suppressive overlapping fire formations, now!" barked Mr Black, into what remained of the execution squad.

Some dropped to one knee and others took a braced, standing posture behind them. Laying down volley after volley, of hot lead, until none of the abominations were left intact.

"Cease fire, cease fire, I SAID STOP!" ordered Mr Black removing his respirator.

He bent over panting, trying to catch his breath and regain his composure.

"Fan out, we need an ID on our man," ordered the squad leader Mr Black.

The remaining members of the squad, spread out nervously, looking among the dead and dying for a positive ID, of the most dangerous quarry possible, the Rudra.

"No sign sir, it, it's like he vanished sir," voiced one of the guards, almost choked by fear and shock.

"Keep looking," barked Black, to the squad.

"Sir we've checked over them all, he's not here" repeated the stunned guard.

"We have to f..." began Black, interrupted mid-sentence, by a chillingly dry voice, that appeared to come from everywhere at once. A chirpy, British accent.

"Cheery ho chaps," mocked the cool voice of the Rudra, and just like the dawn, he was gone, leaving bodies and confusion, in his playful wake.

San Diablo, the devils haven.

CHAPTER 14.

"Sir! somethings moving this way, something big," said agent Sophia, responding to a proximity alert on her vambrace screen.

"Replay image," ordered Rico, switching into a higher mode of alertness. The smile though, returned to his face.

"Something big, eh?" said Rico, leaning closer to the footage replay.

"What was that?" asked Rico, rubbing his eyes with his thumb and index finger. He scrunched his face up, wrinkling his tired eyes. He returned his attention to the screen.

Team Alpha, gathered around the illuminated vambrace of agent Sophia.

A very large humanoid shape, moved slowly across the frame. Something big, around seven feet tall and around four feet broad, with the head of a bull and large, front curved horns, where a man's head should normally be.

The horrifying and mutated form of the minitour like creature, was covered with thick, bloodstained black fur, filthy from the dank old mine.

Commander Rico watched on, mouth agape for only a moment, then shook himself and turned his head to Sophia.

"How long?" he asked, urgently.

"Five, maybe six minutes" replied Sophia, in a slightly stunned tone.

"O'Hara, power up that suit of yours," Rico paused, "Let's see what it can do" continued the commander, to the muscle agent of the team.

"Team Alpha?" asked the commander.

"AAhruuu" grunted his team, pumped and ready for combat.

"Take position. Kill first, ask questions later" ordered Rico.

Silently and swiftly, team Alpha took up tactical positions, in the dark gloom of that enigma of a mine.

Crouching behind the lower half of an ancient ruined statue, of a male soldier, Sophias third eye crown, flashed white and then blue.

The shards of metal, orbiting the incredible killing machine, merged Infront of her, transforming from many, into one, as the needles became a sword.

A katana of incredible strength and an unimaginably sharp edge.

Sophia crouched, ready for action, sword drawn parallel to her body, with both hands on the hilt.

She gripped the shaft of the sword and looked back at Rico, with the kind of love that makes the sun rise. She would die before anything, would happen to him she thought, bringing her breath, again under her conscious control, she prepared for battle.

O'Hara twisted a metal sleave on her huge left forearm. Her body armour glowed red, as if lit from behind.

A smooth 'whirring' noise, came from deep under her body armour, as servo units powered up. Mechanically enhancing the powerful agent's, already considerable strength. Over one hundred times more brawn was now available, to the one-woman army, known only as agent O'Hara. The formidable agent, tucked into a recess in the wall, then braced herself for the coming storm.

Code named Sharky, climbed the elaborately carved tunnel wall, like a spider climbing its web.

Folding backwards, she climbed further onto the ceiling of the ancient tunnel, clinging by her ancles and elbows, and facing the floor. The deadly Sharky, licked her lips in anticipation, of a worthy foe at last.

Rico opened fire, spitting slugs of hot lead, into the dark void and the approaching danger.

The huge creature lurched towards them; bullets ripped through the minotaur's body, without even slowing it down.

The monstrous creature turned its huge, bull like head, towards the gunfire and launched into its own attack mode.

Moving much faster, than should be possible for something that big, the minotaur ran towards the commander, like a freight train.

Agent O'Hara leapt into action. She slammed shoulder first into the creature's side, sending the creature off course, as it staggered slightly sideways.

O'Hara grunted, as she pushed harder against the minotaur. If she could push the beast against the wall, they could swarm it, the creature's size would mean nothing pinned between the Hammer and the anvil, of team Alpha.

The enormous minotaur creature, reached down and grabbed the powerful agent by her webbing, pulling her feet off the ground. O'Hara still held fast to the minotaur's thigh, squeezing hard, she twisted violently at the waist, buckling the knee and hip of the monstrous beast.

Sharky leapt from her position on the tunnel ceiling, landing firmly on the minotaur's shoulders, she grabbed the horns of the beast man, and pulled hard, to reign the minotaur, towards the advantage of the wall.

The minotaur stumbled slightly, then reached up over head, grabbing agent Sharky by the face and throwing her into the opposite wall of the tunnel. She crashed with a thud, into the carved stone, then crumpled to her knees. Winded for a moment, then sprung back to her feet. Like a panther on the hunt, she returned to the aid of her team.

The sight of the gigantic beast, punching agent O'Hara and sending her to the ground, sent the super human agent into a frenzy of violent rage.

She pulled a long ceremonial dagger, an heirloom of her lineage, from her knee-high boot, and slashed viciously into the creature.

Sharky became a flash of Steel and blood, as she delivered blow, after blow, of deadly cuts, all over the beast.

The minotaur roared in pain, as cuts so deep that tendons were severed and bone was chipped, rained down on him, from the deadly rage of agent Sharky.

Sophia, sword raised above her, ran into the battle, her katana sword shimmered in a flash of fury, against the gloom. The song of steel, sliced through the air and it echoed and rang, against the hard tunnel walls.

Sophia leapt into the air, her back arched as she filled herself with air, ready to cleave at the beast. Her sword arced through the air with all the Fury she could use, and came down hard, severing one of the creature's horns, to a stump.

The minotaur recoiled in pain, holding the bloodied stump with both hands. O'Hara, conscious again, ran into the furious battle, enraged by the savage power of the minotaur.

She clasped her arms around the monster's muscular waist, yanking it up, onto the very tips of its toes.

O'Hara the powerhouse, arched her back and slammed the minotaur, face first into the ground. Sophia sliced through the air, once more and then through the creature's neck, decapitating the hell beast, with a blur of violence.

The minotaur's headless body, twitched and jerked, just for a second and then suddenly, sat bolt upright and grabbed agent Sophia, by the throat.

"It's still alive!" exclaimed commander Rico, gun drawn and firing hot lead, into the beasts hairy, muscular torso.

The bullets did nothing, but add to the holes and lacerations, that now covered the impossible creature.

"I got this! move aside," shouted Sharky, wielding Sophias Katana overhead.

Her eyes widened with fury, as she removed the creature's forearm, releasing agent Sophia from the filthy grip of the minotaur.

 Sharky, stabbed the blade of the katana, into the ground Infront of Sophia.

"Do your thing sister Sophia," said Sharky, backing away from the vibrating sword, with anticipation and violent expectation.

"Thank you, sister Sharky," returned Sophia, with a wry smile.

The light on Sophias forehead, flashed to blue again. Her sword continued to vibrate and shake, as agent Sophia rose to her feet.

 The katana vibrated furiously, as the metal blade separated into three flat, round, blades. Deadly sharp and spinning, like circular saw blades in the mill, they sped towards the beast, severing its remaining arm and both legs, at the will of Sophia.

 The severed head, body and limbs of the minotaur thrashed and writhed on the tunnel floor, still trying to attack and fight.

The large, severed bull head of the minotaur, bayed loudly, the beast was still alive. Cursed with immortality, the minotaur clung to an existence of utter pain.

"O'Hara," said the commander, "Put it out of its misery," ordered Rico, to the phenomenal agent O'Hara.

O'Hara's servo units whirred and clicked, as she lifted her foot up high. Looking down at the baying head of the minotaur under boot, she inhaled and in a single merciful and violent act of compassion, she stamped hard on the creature's head, destroying the brain and removing any notion, of pain from the creature.

San Diablo, the devils haven.

CHAPTER 15.

Suarez knelt sobbing and laughing, at the entrance of the mine shaft.

"Betrayer... murderer... you're going to Hell, Hell, Hell!" whispered the giggling and mocking voice of agent Sophia, deep within his shattered mind.

"Come and get me," continued the voice, seductively this time, not menacing, but inviting.

Suarez, elated by the power of his lust, rose to his feet.

He followed the smooth voice into the darkness, of the mine shaft. Blindly in pursuit of the object of his, all-consuming, desire to have Sophia by force, if necessary, but by God, he would murder Rico and take Sophia, or he would die trying, but there would be no turning back, it would happen now, either way.

"I'm going to get you bitch," mumbled Suarez, through his agony of longing.

"I'm gonna get you, so good Puta," continued the mad man, through trembling ghost like lips.

"Come and get me, I'm over here," teased the voice of Sophia, from deep within the dark, shaft tunnel.

"Is everyone ok?" asked commander Rico, shining a torch. Checking himself and his team for injuries. He put a concerned hand on O'Hara's shoulder, and shinned a soft blue light, onto her badly bruised face. He turned his light and attention, to the gash on the back of Sharky's head.

"Sound off," ordered commander Rico.

"Sophia, I'm ok sir," sounded agent Sophia.

"O'Hara, Fine sir," mumbled O'Hara, through swollen lips and closed eyes.

"Sharky, ok," winced Sharky, trying to hide her obvious discomfort.

"Like hell you are! Re-group in the lab! We can press on after we take a look at those injuries. What the hell, was that thing?" asked the commander, leading the way back up the tunnel.

He put his arm around Sharky, to help stabilise the wounded agent.

"I am not so weak commander," she said stubbornly, while removing the commander's arm from her shoulder, gently.

"Let me walk please commander," she asked.

"As you wish Sharky" said Rico, almost choked with admiration.

Sharky walked backwards to help Sophia walk the dazed agent O'Hara.

The broad agent was in the middle of Sophia and Sharky. All had their weapons drawn, ready for any Suprises.

They followed commander Rico, back up the elaborately carved, ancient passage way, back towards the Meth lab.

They could re-group and lick their wounds, look at all the data from Sophia's spies and try to figure out their next move. They made their way slowly, to the relative safety of the Meth lab.

Sophia cleared one of the long benches and helped Sharky, get the wounded O'Hara up onto it.

Rico began dragging whatever could be dragged, to the two entrances. Blocking them up hastily, before re-joining his team. He fixed a florescent tube glowstick, to the wall above O'Hara, bringing a Pristine light to the makeshift surgery.

O'Hara sat up and coughed violently, blood spattered from her bruised, but brave mouth. The upper section of her body armour, breast plate, had dented under the force of the minotaur's punch, causing massive internal bleeding. Sharky put a hand on O'Hara's arm, in an attempt to get the agent to lie down, but to no avail.

The incredible agent O'Hara, grabbed at her breast plate, and in an incredible feat of strength, pulled the armour apart. She gasped a deep, full breath in, then collapsed into the arms of Sharky. Agent Sharky lay the unconscious body of O'Hara, back on the bench with care.

"She's haemorrhaging, do something," sobbed Sharky to Sophia.

"Already on it," replied Sophia, pulling out a large hypodermic syringe, filled with a thick, and glowing, metallic liquid.

She bit off the safety bung, exposing the sharp hollow point of the needle and held it a loft for a moment, before slamming the needle hard between O'Hara's large, pale breasts.

"She will need five minutes for the nano bots to establish," began agent Sophia.

"What do you mean, Nano bots?" inquired commander Rico, puzzled.

"Nano bots sir, tiny microscopic robots. They can repair damage, stop internal bleeding and even carry out surgery, by combining themselves in pre-programmed movements," explained Sophia.

"Like pixels, kind of?" Added Rico, amazed.

"Yes commander," said Sophia blushing under his gaze.

"Standard issue?" asked Rico, knowingly.

"My invention actually commander. O'Hara will be better than new in a matter of minutes." she continued, a little flushed at the attention.

"Well done, Sophia. You blow me away," said Rico returning his attention to O'Hara.

"If only," thought Sophia, blushing intensely.

"Sophia, examine the footage from your spies, lets figure this shit out," ordered the commander, double checking his weapon.

Deep within the tunnel complex, the severed hand of the decapitated minotaur, scratched at the cold dusty floor with blind fingers.

The severed legs, twitched and jerked back to life. The crushed face and head, slowly returned to their original shape, as if inflated from behind.

The burst eyes, returned a new to the creature's hideous face. The severed limbs slid along the tunnel floor, as if magnetised, towards the beast's torso.

Its body jerked, as detached limbs re-joined the quartered minotaur.

The head snapped back into place, re-joined by the rapid healing power of the creature.

The minotaur took a large spasm of breath, and the red eyes of the minotaur, snapped open once again.

"Sophia, check on Sharky. She has a gash on her head, and she won't let me look." said Rico, through a chuckle.

"I know what she's like sir," said Sophia, sliding her hand briefly, down the muscular commander's arm, then turned quickly away.

She moved cautiously toward Sharky, who was stood holding the hand of the unconscious agent O'Hara.

The indicator on agent Sophias vambrace, flashed white and blue and then solid red, alerting Sophia to a problem, a big problem.

"Sir, he's back and headed this way," whispered Sophia to Rico, now running to her position.

She lifted the screen on her vambrace, showing the commander the footage, of the risen minotaur; moving swiftly through the passageway towards them.

"Positions!" ordered Rico, bracing his assault rifle to his shoulder.

Sharky stayed where she was, next to O'Hara, her love.

Sophia, next to her commander, drew her katana from the air. Shards of metal tools and spent ammunition shells, rattled and left the ground, poised to dart under the control, of agent Sophias third eye.

"Protect O'Hara at all costs," ordered commander Rico, through clenched teeth and fiery eyes.

"No agent left behind!" Snarled agent Sharky, poised like a coiled cobra.

The stitches Sophia had put in, were giving her secret pain and heightened intensity. She bared her teeth, ready to protect O'Hara, or die at her feet.

"I'm ready, let the bastard come!" She snarled, pistol and dagger drawn ready.

The Firey agent Sharky, looked like a giant and deadly praying mantis, in the low light of the lab.

A solid pine bench, flew through the Meth lab, smashing against the back wall, above the motionless agent O'Hara.

The metallic detritus hovering in the air, sped towards the minotaur at lightning speed. The enormous minotaur roared in pain, as it dropped to one knee in the doorway, peppered with holes and shards of angry metal. The creature threw a heavy wooden chest across the room, slamming it hard into agent Sophia.

Rico, still firing at the minotaur, ran to her position and knelt next to her, checking her pulse. All the time squeezing the trigger and spitting bullets into her bestial assailant.

Ricos assault rifle jammed, rendering the weapon useless. He dropped the fire arm and, in the blink of an eye snatched his pistol and fired a hot bullet, straight into the creature's eye. Stopping the beast, temporarily.

Sharky roared and ran at the minotaur, emptying her side arm full clip, in to the minotaur's thick, muscular chest.

She arched her dagger, high above her head and slammed the cruel blade, into the minotaur's huge thigh.

The minotaur roared in pain, as it grabbed at the lithe agent Sharky by her head, snapping Sophia's stitches, as he threw the screaming agent, flying through the air.

Sharky braced for impact as best she could, anticipating, the hard, cold stone of the wall, but instead, felt the soft and warm, touch of O'Hara.

Sharky opened her eyes tentively, to be the first to see the new agent O'Hara.

"Are you ok?" boomed O'Hara, her body had altered dramatically, in the absence of observation. The Nanobots had repaired O'Hara perfectly, but deep within the dark of the mine, was an ancient and secret power.

The mine, was no mine, it was an ancient Mayan pyramid, built on top of the hell gate. An area on the earth, where the barrier between earth and hell, is at its thinnest. The incredible, but unpredictable power of the gate, made many things happen. Many, evil, terrible mutations, of men and beast, happened from it and then, that same power, gave the Nanobots in O'Hara, limitless resource and power to rebuild her into a terrible and beautiful, new form.

The powerful mutations, reformed the short O'Hara, into a towering, eight feet, of sheer and utter muscle. Seeming to fill the room, O'Hara gently put agent Sharky on the ground.

"I'm fine now," she said, throwing her arms around the waist of the she hulk, agent O'Hara.

The minotaur charged head down, towards the huge agent, its greatest threat in the room. It lunged at O'Hara, hoping to swiftly dispatch the powerful mutation.

O'Hara grabbed the minotaur by the horns and buckled them sharply to the side, off balancing the enormous brute.

She threw her bulk down on top of him, sprawling the savage beast face down in the dust. She swiftly scrambled to the minotaur's back, taking the superior wrestling position.

O'Hara slid a forearm under the thrashing minotaur's throat, then the powerful agent rolled to her back and wrapped her huge, muscular legs, around and under its large hairy shins.

She had the minotaur, right where she wanted him, in her vice like grip. Controlling the back, she hooked her left arm crease, with her right hand and her left hand, behind the beast's head. The rear naked choke, was locked in.

"Good night sweet prince," mocked O'Hara, as she squose hard, tensing her huge bicep and cutting off any blood, to the creature's brain.

O'Hara, growled savagely and twisted with the minotaur's head. She pulled the beasts head off, from its shoulders, with an astonishing display of power and brute strength.

Its head was still baying, as she threw it across the room, for Rico to finish. Rico yanked his Tanto knife, from within his webbing and plunged the super sharp blade, into the face of the minotaur, over and over again, until the bovine face of the minotaur, was no more than steak tata, splattered all over the floor.

Sharky and Rico, leapt into action, blades ringing as they sliced the creature to pieces. That alone would not kill the beast, not that close to the hell gate, but they could contain the creature, long enough to think.

San Diablo, the devils haven.

CHAPTER 16.

Sophias third eye crown, shone brightly, as her eyes
snapped open. The nimble agent flipped upwards,
landing through the arc, to her feet. Her eyes glowed
white, as if lit up from within. She straightened out her
arm, to spread out her fingers.

Everything metalic rose silently into the air, merging
and melting together, flattening out, into thin plates, of
shiny metal. She flung her arms forward, sending the flat
metal squares, toward the remains of the minotaur.

By a single thought from Sophia, the metalic sheets
wrapped the dismembered remains, of the seemingly
immortal, beast man. Like a pile of possessed Christmas
presents, rattling along the cold, dusty floor.

Team Alpha stood for a moment, breathing deeply,
composing themselves and looking blankly at each other,
then all turn again and stared in amazement and
confusion, at the new and improved, agent O'Hara.

"Did you do this?" asked commander Rico, addressing the puzzled Sophia.

"There were only enough Nanobots available, to repair our sister. This is impossible," spurted agent Sophia.

"Unless, there is a serious amount of power here and serious radiation, available to do this," said Sophia, slipping into thought.

"Like a nuclear power plant or something?" offered Sharky, still smiling up at O'Hara.

"More like, warp power! The unstable warp energy, of inter dimensional jumping, but I thought that was a myth," continued Sophia, deep in thought.

"Sophia, what are you talking about?" asked Sharky confused.

"For us laypersons, please" suggested the commander.

"It's not a myth, I've seen it!" boomed the deep voice, of agent O'Hara.

The room became silent, as if the air itself was waiting for O'Hara, to continue.

"I remember looking down at myself on the table, how hard you all tried, and how hard you cried," said agent O'Hara, gently brushing agent Sharkys cheek with an enormous, curled finger.

"I saw this place long ago, it was like a forest, green and crisp, not a desert at all... Then they came, with their weapons and their lust for power. They travelled hundreds of miles to this place, led by celestial events in the night sky. A super Nova event, most likely, opened a narrow portal, between earth and... and hell.

The Mayans built a pyramid over the cave of wishes and increased the power, of the chaotic warp with human sacrifice. In exchange for powerful soldiers like our friend here." O'Hara gestured to the pile of metal parcels, rocking and jumping, in the corner.

"They would perform intricate blood rituals, to entice a demonic entity, into a willing vassal. The transformations and mutations were horrific and powerful, but short lived. The possessed host, could not sustain the presence of such a creature for long, without mutating beyond usefulness and finally death.

More and more sacrifices were made and more and more hideous abominations were spawned. Eventually the big draught came and the lush green forest, retreated to the desert. This land became corrupted, by the seduction of evil and became cursed, by the greed of man.

 What should have been remembered, became forgotten, and over the centuries, the pyramid was devoured by the ravenous, desert sand. That's why he built the prison here! That's the experiment! He's trying to raise hell on earth, he isn't the warden, he's one of those things, a demon; and he's trying to summon an army of demons, he's trying to alter the prisoners, to be able to contain the monsters... Oh shit sir, we've got to stop him," said agent O'Hara., looking down, into the startled face of commander Rico.

"What are your orders, commander?" said agent Sharky, standing to attention.

"Well unless you have any objections, I suggest we get the Fuck out of here, we can radio HQ for Malone and wait here for back up, or more orders to pursue... sound good team?" asked the commander sarcastically.

"As you command!!!" snapped all three agents, trusting totally, in Ricos ability to lead them out of that god damned pyramid.

"How you doing agent?" asked commander Rico, putting his hand softly, on Sophia's arm.

"You took quite a hit "he continued, tenderly.

"I'll live commander, nothing a hot shower and a massage wouldn't put right," teased Sophia.

"Let's get out of here first," half joked commander Rico.

"I'll hold you to that ... sir," continued Sophia, shyly.

She turned blushing and hurried over to the pile, of packaged Minotaur.

Her light flashed and the metal boxes crushed themselves, then scattered to the walls, held fast by electro magnatraction and the genius of agent Sophia.

"Team Alpha, equipment checks," ordered commander Rico.

The team snapped to it, they checked and double checked their weapons and equipment, with expert scrutiny. O'Hara shared the rest of her ammunition between Sharky, Sophia and Rico.

The Nanobot mutation had made the tiny guns useless to her. The mother of pearl handled, desert eagle hand cannon, looked tiny in her enormous, cupped hands, little more than an ornament to her now.

"This is for you now," said O'Hara blushing, handing Sharky the weapon.

"But this was your fathers," protested agent Sharky, spellbound by O'Hara's generosity.

"I can't use it now, it's shrank," joked the giant agent.

"I want you to have it, will you take it... please," continued O'Hara, smiling nervously.

"I will cherish it... like I cherish you," said Sharky, her heart thumping hard in her chest. She was sure that O'Hara could hear it, beating her name.

"Thank you, it is beautiful," said the agent, smiling from ear to ear.

"So are you" said O'Hara, blushing madly.

"Everyone savvy?" asked commander Rico, bringing the atmosphere back to order.

"Eye sir, we are ready," confirmed agent Sharky.

"Yes sir," said Sophia, checking her vambrace screen, making sure they were clear to move.

"Clear sir," agent Sophia said, looking back up to Rico.

"Alpha team... move out," ordered commander Rico, as he strode towards the tunnel entrance.

He moved swiftly to the open tunnel, with agent Sophia. He moved his gun at line-of-sight, Infront and back into the room, allowing line of sight cover for Sharky and O'Hara, should the minotaur surprise them again.

All members of team Alpha, moved stealthily along the corridor, rotating positions for extra vigilance, it took much longer to cover ground that way, but in that part of hell, you got to be alert. They had their fill of the pyramid and its tricks, and were taking no chances. They were getting the hell out of there.

Sargent Suarez, staggered through the dim light of the tunnel, his head heavy with thoughts of love and hate.

A bright, ultraviolet light, shone Infront of the betrayer, hurting his dry eyes and piercing his mind.

He put a hand up in front of his face, shielding his eyes from the painful blue light.

As his eyes grew accustomed to the light, he slowly began to make out the brilliant image, of a woman's form, hovering above the dusty ground.

The apparition moved closer, to the startled sargent.

The fuzzy image became less and less painful to look at and became sharper and sharper, until finally, the true image was revealed to him.

Suarez rubbed his eyes in disbelief, as his addled brain recognised, what his heart already knew.

"My lady" he gasped, dropping to his knees.

He joined his hands together in prayer.

"Hail Mary, full of grace, blessed art thou among women. Mary mother of god, forgive us, us sinners in this our hour of need," offered Sargent Suarez, trembling before the image.

"Don't be afraid Ranaldo," spoke the apparition softly to the crying man, known as Ranaldo Manuelle Suarez.

Suarez looked up at the unreal sight, of the virgin Mary, dressed in blue coverings, just like on his prayer candle, but with Sophias beautiful face. He gasped for a moment, as if in a state of grace.

"I know what you want Ronaldo," said the image, floating serenely before him.

Suarez looked hard at the ghostly Madonna, with a burning desire to conquer, the Holy mother's virginity.

The sight of agent Sophia as the virgin Mary, spiked his animal lust and he began thinking about what he would do to her, by force if necessary.

"You used to be such a good boy too," said the Madonna, moving closer to the aroused sargent.

He stared like a teenage boy, at the figure of the Virgin Mary. His eyes lingered at her hips and breast, with a shaking neck, he lifted his trembling head, to look at the beautiful face of agent Sophia.

His desire for sex, was palpable in the dusty air, he could wait no longer. The grip of lust had crushed what remained, of the man's sanity. He could taste her on his tongue already.

His body stiffened, as he braced himself ready for diabolical action. He darted his hands towards her, attempting to grab her for his own.

The second he tried to touch her, she changed.

Her face transformed in an instant, from the gentle and warm features of Sophia, to that of a monster. Her cheeks were sunken and wrinkled, her mouth open, agape with rage, exposing row after row, of razor-sharp fangs.

The softness of her deep brown eyes, replaced with wide, evil eyes, with no iris. Just the white glow, of angry and terrifying eyes, punctuated with pin hole like pupils.

Her hair stood wildly on end and her clothes became as strips of rags, floating in the ether, like a spider's web in the breeze.

The refined and beautiful form of the virgin, Ave Maria, had become the frightening form of the Bruha, a witch from ancient times, blamed for every misfortune imaginable, since the dark age of conquest.

The terrible form of the Bruha, lunged suddenly towards the petrified, sargent Suarez. Shocked and startled, the disgraced man staggered backwards and fell onto the dark, dusty floor.

He scrambled in the low gloom, desperately feeling in the dust, for his dropped fire arm. Without taking his eyes off the ghostly phantom, he drew his weapon and opened fire, spraying bullets into the empty space, of the gloomy entrance to the mine.

The Bruha changed once more, then vanished into the gloom, leaving Suarez alone, in the dark, dilapidated, entrance to the mine shaft.

The tormented and damned Suarez, full of anger and self-loathing, dashed into the dark tunnel, in pursuit of lust and hate.

Driven by vengeance, the broken man quickened his pace. His breath caught in his bone-dry throat, with a raspy growl. Rico was somewhere near; he could sense him. An animal like instinct took over, as the thrill washed over him, like rain.

"Soon" he thought, shaking on the inside with sadistic arousal.

He could picture agent Sophia in his mind's eye, naked and bound, with the body of commander Rico, watching on as he fucked her.

"Betrayer, your time is neigh...SINNER!!!" the voices had returned to Sargent Suarez. He paid little attention to them, as he reloaded his weapon, with evil, trembling hands.

San Diablo, the devils haven.

CHAPTER 17.

Team Alpha stopped silently in the dark, cold tunnel. The unmistakable sound of gunfire, had stopped them in their tracks. A blur of blue lights darted past them, as agent Sophias drone spies, shot past them to investigate the threat.

The silence in that place was deafening, until it was punctuated by the sound of footsteps, racing towards them, followed, like a shadow, by laughter.

Sophia too late, checked the screen on her vambrace, as the owner of the laugh, was upon them.

Suarez was already on their position; his speed was incredible. High on love, hate and adrenaline, Suarez let fly with the AK47, spitting vengeance, in a storm of hot lead.

"Ha, Ha, get some Rico, get some, get some!" roared the insane, Sargent Suarez, into the gloom.

Ricos thigh gave way and a familiar agony, rushed through his body, up into his brain. He'd been shot, the burning in his leg intensified, as he scrambled to cover.

A line of bullet holes, followed him like footprints in the sand.

"You like that huh? You like that," Suarez was cut off mid word, as the spider drones silently harpooned him, dragging him off the ground.

The spider drones, under the control of Sophia, rapidly hoisted the disgusting Sargent up and slammed him, hard into the tunnel ceiling, only to drop him to the floor.

Sophia sent the thought, for the spider drones to repeat and then turned her attention to the injured commander Rico.

Sophia pulled the personnel med kit, from the rear of Ricos body webbing. Agent Sharky, shone her torch over Sophias shoulder, casting a bright light on commander Ricos thigh.

Sophia cut a square of material away from around the wound and bit the protective cap, from a cigar shaped chrome device.

She looked up at him from her knees and blew out her cheeks.

"One, two" ... began Sophia, holding the device with an over hand grip, close to the wound site, preparing to stab.

"AARGH... you fucker," gasped commander Rico, before quickly regaining his composure.

Sophia plunged the device, deep into the bullet hole. The skin around the wound moved and wriggled, as Sophia felt around, deep within the raw wound.

She looked up again at the commander, and took a sharp breath in, from the side of her mouth.

"Sorry about this sir" she said, shrugging sympathetically, Sophia pressed the end of the device sending a flexible, robotic tentacle, into the skin of commander Ricos leg.

Lit by the tiny robot, tracing the path of the bullet, now lodged deep in commander Ricos thigh. The red dot turned green, indicating the clamp had engaged and dragged the bullet back, through the fresh, painful wound.

Sophia slowly and as gently as she could, removed the blood-soaked slug from the commander's leg. She held it up and passed the bullet, to her commander.

Suarez hit the floor again with a bloody 'Thump', then smashed dead, into the ceiling.

One of the rockets, he stashed from the bike, jostled out of his front webbing and tucked under the dead man's chin. 'Slam,' he dropped again to the ground, then 'Crack' into the ceiling, then 'BANG'!

The shell, slammed into the ground and detonated, on the blood-stained, stone floor.

With the reflexes of a cat, O'Hara stood Infront of the others, arms around them all. She pulled her team in close, instinctively protecting them from the blast.

The heatwave was so intense, that O'Hara's entire skin on her back, had melted and merged with her armour.

The Nanobot's quickly began repairing her, healing her almost instantly.

The pain of burned skin and the immediate healing, would kill a regular person, but there was nothing regular left, about the incredible agent O'Hara, not now.

She put all of her awareness into breathing, putting off the urge to scream, and in so brought herself the precious moments of calm, until the intense pain would subside.

O'Hara let go of her team and winced slightly, as the Nano surgeon's, finished repairing her skin and armour.

Team Alpha watched in horror, as the ceiling began to cave in, right in front of them.

The rockface attached to Sargent Suarez, fell and flattened the man, splashing gore everywhere.

Agent O'Hara, scooped up commander Rico under her arm. The big man looked like a child, in the arms of the hulking agent.

She ran down the tunnel, agents Sharky and Sophia close behind. Rocks and boulders crashing to the ground, at their heels.

Team Alpha, ran full speed down the corridor and jumped sharp right, back into the Meth lab. Just as the tunnel behind them, collapsed.

Clouds of dust filled the lab, forcing them to put their respirators on, until the dust could settle enough to breathe.

Rico walked over to the pile of jumping metal cubes, he stooped over and picked one up, wincing in pain as he straightened. He blew his cheeks out, putting a full stop on the pain.

"Hello again old friend," he said to the piece of minotaur, rattling in its tiny, tin tomb.

He gently placed it back on its pile with the rest of it, then fell on his face, overcome with pain. He quickly tried to get to his feet, angry at himself for the fall.

O'Hara picked him up and placed him on the bench, firmly.

"Stay still, I need to mend this wound sir," scolded Sophia, pulling out another phial of Nano tech liquid. "Whoa, Whoa," protested commander Rico, half sitting up.

"These are different sir; they will only stitch your wound, they won't enhance you like our sister O'Hara," said agent Sophia, reassuring the commander. Sophia injected Ricos leg with the metallic liquid, without warning.

"Son of a...!" blasted Rico.

"Smarts, don't it sir?" sympathised Sophia.

"It did, phew... is that it, done?" asked Rico, already back on his feet.

"Not yet sir," said Sophia, squatting to the ground in front of him, she kissed the exposed site of the wound, with her soft, warm lips.

"There, that's better," she said, looking up at him seductively, then standing, without taking her eyes off his.

"Much," said Rico, checking his leg over, a little flustered.

"See what we can find and use team, let's see what we've got here," said commander Rico, taking stock of his ammunition status. Less than half of his bullets remained, after that long, long night.

"Yes, yes, there is no need for an umbrella at the moment, but I would recommend getting one soon," said special agent Malone, into the receiver of his satellite cell phone.

He hung up the call by folding the phone in half, and handed the secure comms device, back to agent Jeffries.

"He made an appearance?" asked agent Sterling, starting the engine of the sleek, black SUV, suburban.

"Yes, and he caused a wonderful mess for the warden too," said Malone, with a little satisfaction in his voice.

"He's left quite a few bodies in his path, bodies that must be replaced," continued Malone, smiling at Stirling through the rear-view mirror.

"Yes, then we can detect the energy pattern of the transfer and where they hide the, er, 'Professor' sir," said Jeffries excitedly.

He was looking forward to bringing the evil professor down, he had personal reasons, family reasons.

"Thats correct agent," said Malone, clocking Jeffries behaviour and logging it to memory, for now.

"What next then sir?" asked Stirling, from behind the wheel.

"Next we keep a line of sight on the warden, make sure he sees us, ruffle his feathers a little," replied Malone from the rear of the car.

"What about him though sir?" enquired Stirling.

"He will appear when he's ready, but I'm not in a hurry for him. He will prove yet more essential to our plan, I'm sure of it," replied Malone, to the stoic agent Stirling.

"It's one heck of a gamble though sir" said agent Jeffries, hacking into the facilities security footage.

"He really doesn't want us to see this. Last night's footage has been pulled and deleted, but only from the prison mortuary and surrounding complex," said agent

Jeffries, looking up from his hollo screens and rubbing his eyes.

"Then that is where we shall go. Now...agent Stirling, to the prison fridge room, we got us a warden to upset," said Malone, a plan beginning to form in his brilliant mind.

"How so sir?" asked special agent Stirling from the front of the vehicle.

"He doesn't want us to know about last night's little party, or he would have contacted me by now, with us turning up there for a snoop round, he will suspect an informant and things will really get colourful around here," smiled Malone, to the other two agents.

The three CIA men, drove slowly around the prison highway, taking in as much data as they could, just by observing the guards, they got all they needed.

"There are much less of them around us, he can't spare the assets for now," said Stirling, to the car in general.

"Then all is going to plan," commented Jeffries.

"Yes, it is all unfolding perfectly," said the leader of the team, special agent Malone.

The black SUV, came to a slow halt in front of a
temporary checkpoint, blocking the driveway entrance to
the San Diablo, prison mortuary.

Two guards, armed with military issue M16's,
approached the driver's side window, of the mean
looking, black vehicle.

Three other men, armed with shotguns stood behind the
metal barrier pole. Malone noted, the three men were a
posse of inmates, deputised prisoners from the outer
blocks. Unusual metal enhancements, half concealed
behind tattered uniforms, got the agents attention.

Jeffries began searching through the prison files, from
behind his sunglasses monitor, using his pupils to control
the screen like a computer mouse.

"No entry gentlemen," said the larger of the two-armed
men.

All three agents turned their heads towards the man, at
the same, exact time.

"What happened here, officer?" they said in unison,
throwing the guards attention.

"By orders of the warden," said the guard, stepping backwards half a step, visibly uncomfortable to be near the soulless faces, hidden behind those secret service issue sunglasses.

"What happened here?" repeated the agents, in a flat, yet aggressive tone.

The other guard raised his assault rifle, pointing it at the car. The three deputies, came from behind the makeshift barrier and stood firmly in front of it. They cocked their shotguns, by pumping the handles and stood wide legged and braced, holding the loaded weapons ready.

Malone smiled to himself.

"They, say it by not saying, don't they? Thank you, gentlemen, you've been most helpful" he said, patting his knee with the palm of his left hand.

The agent's car, reversed back a little and parked up. The noise of the engine, came to a halt and the three faceless agents, stepped out of the vehicle straightening their ties. With rehearsed synchronicity, they closed their doors silently and strode menacingly towards the blockade and the guards.

"Put the gun down son, before you hurt yourself, don't you know its rude to point a loaded gun?" said Malone, to the tall guard with the assault rifle.

With the speed of a bullet, special agent Malone, snatched the gun from the startled guard, and tossed it sideways to Stirling, who without taking his eyes off the other guard, caught the weapon and turned it on the man.

"Especially at me," finished Malone.

"We don't get told why, we just get told do, Ya'll take it up with the warden if you must, but Ya'll can't come in here," said the gun less guard, sternly.

An ex-army, Apache gunship helicopter, appeared above the prison mortuary complex and hovered slowly, towards the blockade.

"This is a restricted area, you are not permitted to be here, return to your quarters immediately, or we WILL open fire!" Boomed a stern voice, from the choppers announcement system.

"Like I said Mr Malone" smirked the guard.

"It's, agent Malone," interrupted the tall agent, smoothly.

"Sorry, AGENT Malone, Ya'll take it up with the boss, but Ya ain't getting in there," said the guard, pointing with his thumb behind him, to the sealed off unit.

"Or, he will take it up with me," said Malone, unphased by the helicopter.

"Agent Stirling, could you deal with that please," said special agent Malone, pointing to the chopper.

The black Apache began to rotate, spinning wildly in mid-air under the control of the agents on board computer and the CIA sunglasses. The three agents Stood in the same position, as if unaware of the spinning chopper.

The helicopter landed heavily next to the blockade, with a crash and a bounce.

"Excuse me a moment," said agent Malone, holding up an apologetic finger to the shell-shocked guard, stood Infront of him.

The smile had left the guards face and found its way, as it often did, to special agent Malone.

Malone stormed angrily, towards the downed bird and flung open the pilot's side door.

He pulled himself up and the dazed pilot pulled his revolver, but too late Malone grabbed the man's wrist and snapped his forearm in half, with a figure four arm lock.

Malone dragged the screaming man, half out of the helicopter. The pilot, draped upside down and screaming, witnessed the fury of the big CIA agent. Malone began furiously, stamping on the man's chest and face, switching to savage punches, all over the man and then back to stamping and kicking.

"DONT YOU... EVER... EVER... FUCKING EVER! POINT A FUCKING GUN AT ME.... EVER," roared Malone, his eyes were wide and manic, his teeth bared and primal.

His smooth smart hair, ruffled and messy, from his terrible display of barbarism. He stopped for a moment to catch his breath, before soccer kicking the dead man's body once more.

Malone spat on the man and straightened up, smoothed out his hair, tucked his shirt back into his trousers and put his sunglasses back on, calmly and smoothly.

Malone folded the man back into his seat, the co-pilot reached instinctively, towards his own sidearm, hovering over the holster. Malone glared at the trembling man, who on thinking better, snapped his hand back to his lap.

"Good lad," smiled Malone, with a nod.

Agent Malone, stepped off the gunship and glared at the two officers and their posse. The men all jumped in fear and realisation, then threw their weapons on the driveway floor, as if they were hot to the touch.

He walked past them and without saying a word, the three men got back into the black suburban.

"Who in the hell does he think he is?" said the disarmed guard gruffly.

"It's not who the hell, we think he is, that's for sure Joe," said the other, blowing air out of pursed lips with relief.

The two men gathered themselves together, with a shared sigh of weighty resolution.

"Don't just stand there you dumb sons of bitches," said Joe, running towards the downed helicopter and what remained of her crew.

"Come on!" shouted the first guard, to the three deputies.

The startled men jumped to it and ran towards the chopper, catching up quickly with the guards.

They yanked open the pilot's door, reached over the bludgeoned corpse of the pilot and grabbed the helicopter radio.

"I'm calling it in, something needs to be done about that son of a bitch," mumbled the first guard, shocked with anger and indignation.

"Hello, get me Mr Black!" yawped the man into the radio handset.

"That ought to do it," said Malone to the other two special agents.

"They will be less enthusiastic to use force now," said Stirling, keeping in step with the others.

"Now that they realise, they cannot match our strength, they will become more useful, to us and to our mission," offered Jeffries.

The three faceless agents walked back down the driveway, leaving the SUV parked.

They set off towards the outer prison complex, whistling the National anthem, as they stepped in perfect unison.

A customised, ex-military personnel carrier, came rapidly into the agents view, escorted by two large jeeps, all full of elite armed guards.

The three special agents, without saying a word to one another, stopped motionless in the dusty road. Like cobras sensing prey, they held firm.

"Looks like our rides here," said special agent Malone to the others. A wry, predatory smile, flickered across his face like the dance of shadows and flames.

The convoy of armed guards, drew closer and closer, until coming to a screeching halt, Infront of Malone and his team.

The armed guards, filed out of the truck and jeeps, their black exo armour glimmered in the bright morning sun. These were the best men the warden had, the super elite and super expensive private militia. The 'death makers.

The huge mercenaries, fanned out Infront of the agents, with true military precision.

A single mercenary stood forward of the main body of men and removed his helmet.

"Special agent Malone?" enquired the man, cordially.

Malone nodded silently at the man, in response.

"The warden would like you and your team, to join him for an early lunch, now. If convenient," continued the elite guard, politely yet aggressively.

"And if it's not, convenient?" asked Malone dryly.

The Death maker, walked Straight up to agent Malone, eye to eye. The mercenary smiled at the agent, like the almighty himself.

"Then we will have to make you," said the death maker leader, with a voice like poisoned honey.

"Well then, I'm sure we can free up a little time for an early bite," returned Malone, not taking his eyes off the man.

"I'm truly relieved to hear that special agent, will you and your party, come to ride with me" said the soldier, flatly.

"We would be delighted," said Malone, sensing something familiar about this mercenary.

San Diablo, the devils haven.

CHAPTER 18.

The swell of heavily armed and armoured guards, parted
down the middle, forming an exit path to the death
makers heavily customised jeep.

The upgrades to the vehicle, were like nothing the veteran agent had ever seen. The jeep had eight thick wall, desert wheels, on a flexible chassis, allowing the mercenaries high speed, even over the most rugged of desert terrain.

The vehicle was closed in with thick Chromite armour. The cameras mounted in clusters all over the vehicle, gave the jeep an intimidating, arachnid aesthetic.

Mounted to the rear were two side by side, turret guns, as long as the vehicle itself. Scratched into the black painted Chromite armour, a long line of five bar tally gates, ran in multiple rows covered the entire passenger side of the vehicle.

A running count of customers, for the ferry man.

"This way please gentlemen" said the death makers leader, gesturing with a wave of the hand, towards the passenger side, of the intimidating vehicle. Making sure agent Malone could notice the body count, etched there on.

"Sweet ride son, I had one just like it, when I was your age," said Malone smoothly.

The three CIA men stopped at their chaperones ride and turned back, taking in the view of the elite mercenary squad.

Malone sighed and turned slightly to their escort.

"They're a little fat, aren't they?" whispered agent Malone to the mercenary leader, in a pretend tone of disappointment.

The mercenary looked sideways at the agent, but only with his eyes. Without speaking, he pressed the side of his wrist armour, activating the opening mechanism for the heavy Chromite doors.

The heavy doors, silently snapped open. The four doors opened upward, making the vehicle even more insect like and intimidating.

"After you, gentleman," said the guard, gesturing for the agents to board, the mean looking, sand dancer.

The four of them, got into the cramped interior of that most unique, type of vehicle.

Harness bars, slid out from the sides and above the bucket seats, locking in place with powerful magnets, in front of each agent.

The doors slammed shut and the outside world disappeared, both sound and sight, from view.

"The squad are fat and idle, without a decent war to keep them trim. They are in sound need, of a good fight; and they are rather hoping you, might give them one" said the death maker leader, looking sideways and smiling broadly.

"So, the troops are ready for a challenge then? Good to know," said Malone.

"If you continue to make a storm, you will only get wet," continued agent Malone, now looking side long back at the man.

"Then it's a good thing that we have an umbrella, wouldn't you agree?" replied the man, firing up the super charged engine of the vehicle.

"Silence is a virtue" replied the special agent, with a finger on his lips.

The heavily armoured vehicle hummed, as the powerful engine, fired up in the Nevada desert. Intense blue energy, illuminated the space beneath the vehicles, as the nuclear propulsion units engaged, sending that small convoy of bad asses, speeding off into the distance.

Heading to the outer pentagon, of the San Diablo prison complex, transporting the three CIA special agents, to the demonic overseer of the facility himself, the warden.

Team Alpha stacked up everything they could find, that could be of any use. They began sifting through and sorting the collection of MS13 stockpiled weapons and equipment, abandoned in the lab.

"Sharky, what is the water situation?" asked commander Rico, to the smiling agent Sharky.

"Sir, we only got about one litre between us, but we got piss cleaner sir, three packs," replied the athletic agent.

"What does that even mean Sharky?" continued Rico, shaking his head.

"It means Sir, that we got enough nice water for tonight, but after that, it's the nasty, stinky, recycled piss water, so, sip that shit my family, make it last," answered Sharky, wrinkling her face up and juddering, laughing at the seriousness of their situation.

"Let's see what we got here," said the commander, inspecting the row of items, sifted through by Sophia and Sharky.

Agent O'Hara growled at the rattling heap, of metal boxes, containing the defeated Minotaur. The beast was easily cowed to silence, by the hulking, Alpha female.

O'Hara snorted, then stood back up and continued Searching for a weapon, more suited to her own unique needs.

Commander Rico walked from wall to wall, inspecting the long row of armament, salvaged from the lab, by the resourceful crew.

An impressive haul of rifles, hand guns and assault weapons, accompanied by piles of bullets, grenades, swords and knives, flares and a two-way radio comms.

He winced in pain, from the wound on his thigh. He had almost forgotten about it, until he tried to squat down to grab the walkie talkie, but then the intense pain from the healing wound hit him, like a kick in the balls.

The commander staggered slightly backwards, and his leg buckled beneath his pride, sending the staunch commander Rico, to the ground. He gripped the wall blindly, in an attempt to get up, only to lose consciousness altogether.

The three agents, sprung to Ricos unconscious body, asleep as it were, on the dusty, lab floor.

The sleeping commander stirred and with a sharp grunt, opened his eyes.

He was lying on one of the long, truss tables come hospital bed. He felt like shit, like a hundred hangovers, his leg felt cold and numb.

He felt a sensation like weightless flight, as agent Sophia administered more anaesthetic, into the canular in his arm.

She put her cool hand, onto his warm forehead and, he looked straight at her smiling.

"Sophia," said the injured commander, before falling back to sleep again.

Commander Rico had been unconscious for two whole days, agent Sophia had kept him medically asleep, to Perform emergency surgery on him and needed the stubborn veteran still and calm to help facilitate, in the healing process.

The three super human agents, had kept themselves busy in his absence, indeed, they still had much to do, to be ready. Before the commander would be woke up. The agents knew, he would demand that they move out from the meth lab and head out, down the dark shaft and try to find a way out, of the ancient, forgotten pyramid, somewhere in the harsh Nevada desert.

"How much longer sister?" asked agent O'Hara to Sophia.

"We need to set off soon, will he be ready?" asked Sharky.

They all knew that what food and water, they had found, would not last long. The sooner they could get moving, the better.

With no way of contacting HQ and no way of getting in, thanks to sargent Suarez, they knew rescue was not even possible. They had to escape and they had to do it now.

"Another day... max" replied agent Sophia, to the urgent Sharky.

"Any movement from your spies?" enquired Sharky.

"All's quiet, there's been nothing since our friend here," answered agent Sophia, while forming metal components, from some of the weapons salvaged by the team.

The blue light on her forehead, flickered intensely, like morse code from a torch, as thought became action and metals changed form.

Sophia was able to command the electromagnetic signature, of all metallic objects with her neuro intensifier head piece.

She could change the structure and shape of objects and agent Sophia, the mistress of metal, worked feverishly on commander Ricos leg.

"He's expecting you this time," said the mercenary to the agents as a whole.

The jeep came to a sudden, but smooth stop at the entrance to the outer block. The gate was held open, by one of the death maker mercenaries.

"Now agent Malone? Team? Allow me to get the door," said the hulking leader of the death makers, flicking an overhead toggle switch.

The doors snapped smoothly up, into the open position and their harnesses released. Sliding instantly back into their position, out of the way of the disembarking agents.

The four of them exited the vehicle, in silence and synchronicity.

The other jeep and armed truck, flanked them from a distance, heavy weapons on display, ready to respond to their superiors will, without question, or hesitation.

The three CIA men, observed the mercenaries show of strength for a moment, enjoying the discipline on show. A refreshing change from the rabble, under the warden's sloppy charge.

"They will get their fight general," whispered agent Stirling to the mercenary.

"Let me know when, colonel." whispered the man in return.

"Shall we, gentlemen?" said the mercenary leader, marching towards the guard and the entrance to the outer block and the endless viewing balcony, leading to the warden's office.

The guard at the gate saluted them and moved to one side, leaving the entrance clear, for the agents to step through.

"Malone," said the mercenary, he held a hand up while fishing in a large pocket, in his front webbing.

"These will be quicker," he added, handing the agents what looked like, a thick shoe sole each.

"Much obliged," said special agent Stirling, speaking for the team.

The death maker leader waved a signal, to more of the mercenaries, positioned strategically in checkpoints leading to the viewing balcony and the long, and monotonous, corridor to the warden's office.

The mercenaries on the first level, were joined by more prison officers. Those on the upper level and final checkpoint, were accompanied by a group of tall, hooded figures.

Their thick red cowls, fully obscured their identity, gender or species, from the view of the CIA agents.

The three special agents swiftly and silently, moved through checkpoint after checkpoint, absorbing as much data from their surroundings and their escorts as possible, to analyse through the CIA data base later.

The sunglasses on the three agents, had a full three hundred- and sixty-degrees, shared line of sight. Each could see what the others could, and everything seen was logged and recorded remotely, by the incredible black SUV. A mobile CIA HQ, equipped with all the equipment and tech, that the three super spies could use. Way more than they would ever need.

Behind the black lens of the agents' sunglasses, faces were being framed and records were being pulled, equipment was identified and concealed weapons were highlighted, by the smart hard ware, built into the agent's glasses.

The faceless agents traversed the metal stairs, up to the upper level silently. A red robed figure, moved as if gliding, towards the open entrance, to greet the men.

"This way please," announced the figure, in an icy, synthetic, woman's voice.

The figure turned and gracefully, sped towards the heavy metal door, leading to the long corridor.

More of the identical hooded figures, moved effortlessly into formation, flanking the walking agents.

Agent Jeffries sniffed at the air and stopped suddenly, Malone and Stirling stopped immediately, in step with special agent Jeffries. The three agents looked up slightly, for only a heartbeat and then, without saying a word, set off again in unison.

Step for step, they made their way to the heavy metal barrier door, and with mechanical synchronicity, climbed the three steps. They went through the guarded entrance and into the seemingly, endless corridor.

The special agents had only taken a few steps, before the door slammed shut behind them. The click of the lock sliding into place, echoed down the corridor.

 The three men pulled the sole like objects from their pockets and with a subtle twist and pull, the devices opened up like books, in their hands.

The three agents dropped the devices on the corridor floor and stepped on them, as if standing on footprints in the sand.

 An intense red light, shone from under the footprint like devices, lifting the devices, and the agents, three inches off the ground.

 The hum from the magnetic manipulation, fluttered the air beneath the hoverboards, making the space around the agent's throb, with the self-perpetuating energy, of the death maker hover boards. The three CIA agents pushed slightly downwards with their toes, directing the magnetic force of the board.

They sped down the corridor, accelerating rapidly and gracefully, around the long perimeter of the inside viewing Gentree, of the outer pentagon block.

The agents moved silently around the first corner and out of view, the low rumble of the hover boards propulsion, followed them like a shadow, until it too, had passed.

"Spider drone discovery!" said agent Sophia, excitedly.

"What we got?" asked O'Hara, picking up a helicopter midi gun, found hidden in a side chamber, off the main tunnel.

"Looks like another false wall," reported Sophia to her sister agents.

"Let's go babe," said Sharky, patting agent O'Hara on her huge, muscular thigh.

The two agents checked over their weapons and each other's modified body armour, in turn.

Sophia tossed one of the walkie talkies to Sharky, with a beaming smile.

"Stay in contact, I'll watch over the commander," said Sophia, from commander Ricos bed side.

"Have the drone flash when we are near. See you later Sophia," said O'Hara, back to agent Sophia, and the unconscious commander Rico.

The two agents disappeared into the darkness of the pyramid tunnel in search of the flashing drone and the hidden chamber. They had investigated many such rooms hidden from the main tunnel. Some recent, knock up attempts at false walls and some ancient and better concealed chambers, all were used to cache weapons and goods, of varying types from antiquity.

The tunnel was littered with rubble from the smashed open, discoveries from previous treasure hunts.

O'Hara and Sharky, stealthily picked their way down the tunnel, ahead they saw the white flashing light, of the spider drone, illuminating the hieroglyphs on the walls and ceiling.

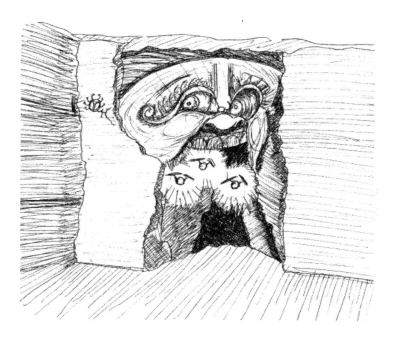

 The statues of Mayan Gods and warriors, appeared to
dance in the flickering light, against the ornate tunnel,
walls and ceiling.

Sharky and O'Hara, cautiously approached the flashing
spider drone, ready for anything.

The sensitive equipment in Sophia's drones, gave them
the ability to check for unstable rock faces. Using
sysmick, geo Phys systems, they could map any voids
within three feet, when in spider drone mode, and this
drone had detected a big void and possibly another

ancient, cache of weapons, that Sophia could make use of.

Agent Sharky waved at the spider drone, signalling back to Sophia to move the drone to safety and to watch over them, in case she was needed to rush to the aid, of her sister agents.

The drone leapt to the opposite wall and O'Hara began tapping the section of masonry, listening for the change in sound, looking for the hollow. Agent O'Hara placed both enormous hands, on the ornately carved section of wall.

Tremendous force travelled up from the ground, through the agent muscular legs and core. O'Hara braced and sent a powerful blast of strength, into her outstretched hands, pushing a large hole into the ancient wall, and exposing a large room, hidden for millennia, behind a cunning disguise.

Dust billowed out from the opening, filling the tunnel with a thick, grey cloud of rubble and dust.

 The body armour under agent Sharkys chin, blinked twice. The air quality had triggered the agent's respirator, and within a fraction of a second, sections of armour had joined themselves, into a full face and head, visored protective helmet. A respirator mask, locked into position over agent Sharkys mouth and nose.

The Nanobots sharing O'Hara, quickly built a carbon filter mask over her face, followed quickly by a protective helm of her own.

"Man, that's cool," said agent Sharky, in awe of O'Hara and her Nanobot army.

Sharky signalled to the drones, by drawing a circle in the air with her index and forefinger, then pointed into the dark opening, with the same index finger.

Five drones quickly flew, into the darkness of the chamber.

"No heat signatures, or signs of movement, air quality not bad, but keep the masks on, over," crackled the distant voice of agent Sophia, over the salvaged walkie talkie.

"Roger that sister, going in," replied agent Sharky, from behind her visor.

Sharky ran a finger around the lower edge of her visor, switching on a line of LED lights, framing the front section of her helmet.

O'Hara activated a large red glow stick, and the two women stepped out of the tunnel and into the hidden room. The darkness of the Chamber, hung from the lights like a cloak around a coach man.

San Diablo, the devils haven.

CHAPTER 19.

Commander Rico sat bolt up, from his prolonged induced state, of deep sleep and opened his eyes, to the warm sight of the beautiful agent Sophia, standing at his side.

 She smiled warmly at him, as he reached out to her with an open hand.

"Sophia... I... I... I, thank you Sophia," he smiled at her with such warmth, that she felt like she would melt into him, then looked down.

His eyes became puzzled and narrow, then, with a sudden sharp intake of breath, they widened. He looked up at Sophia, in almost shock and disbelief

"What happened to my leg?" enquired Rico, staring at a shiny metallic prosthetic limb, where his own leg used to be. The last he knew there was an actual leg there, but now from the hip down, his entire leg was robotic.

He looked back up, at the distressed face of agent Sophia. Moved by her compassion, he gently lifted her chin with his finger, and looked lovingly back into her deep, dark eyes.

"I know you would have saved it, if that was possible I would no doubt have died, if not for your diligence," he said gently.

"So," said commander Rico, trying out the new leg. "Care to de-brief me?" he continued, pulling the cannular from his hand and jumping to his feet.

"You've been out for three days, sir. The Nano bots in your leg, replicated your tissue as they were supposed to, but instead of normal, healthy tissue, they mutated horribly and in such a short time. Your leg was completely rotten from the calf down, I... I had to amputate the entire leg, before the corrupted Nanobots, could spread to the rest of you," Sophia's voice choked for a moment, as if the heavy words, could no longer leap from her throat.

"We almost lost you... sir," she continued, steadying herself, with a slow exhalation.

"We fashioned your new leg, from gun metal mainly, each joint is connected to your nervous system, by tiny golden threads, attached to your nervous system and your brain stem," Sophia smiled again, at the rugged commander.

"Did you do all this with your" ... Rico paused trying desperately to find the right word, he was so in awe of her and didn't want to look foolish, especially not in her incredible presence.

"Erm, Crown," he said hopefully.

Sophia nodded, bashfully.

"Sophia... you're the most incredible person I've ever met, thank you," said the blushing commander.

"Anything for you, commander," she said smiling broadly. She turned her blushing face away slightly and turned away shyly.

She stopped and turned back to him; his muscular frame was lit up from behind by the bright glow stick. She almost buckled at the sight of him, she felt that he was the very reason for sight and the cause of her own eyes, she panged for him deeply and found sustenance in his presence.

"Sir I..." Sophia began to say, until the crackle of the walkie talkie broke her concentration and courage.

"Sophia come in... over," crackled the unmistakable voice of agent Sharky.

"Sophia here, what is it sister?" asked Sophia, into the salvaged communicator.

"Sophia, are you getting this?" asked Sharky, in a tone of utter disbelief.

Agent Sophia held her vambrace up to her chest, watching live on the smart screen, the footage and data from the spider drones in the hidden chamber.

"What in the?" asked agent Sophia, as if in a trance.

Commander Rico gently took the radio, from agent Sophia.

"Commander Rico here, we are on route to your position, over," said the commander, grinning at Sophia.

"Well, we'd better check that out," said Rico turning to Sophia.

He faked a stumble and braced himself against the table.

"A little help?" he asked, putting his arm around agent Sophia's athletic shoulder.

"My pleasure" she purred, threading her arm under his, and clutching tight, to his rock-hard, toned waist.

O'Hara smiled behind her visor.

"Ricos awake!" she exclaimed joyfully and with relief in her voice.

"I knew he'd make it," she continued.

"HAH, I knew she would make him make it," laughed agent Sharky, knowingly.

"That's incredible, I can still feel the ground, how?" commander Rico asked Sophia, stopping momentarily to look at his robotic foot. His toes had been replaced with sickle like talons, which wriggled as he watched.

"I overlapped your nervous system, with tiny pieces of copper alloy, you can feel sensations of temperature and texture and even experience touch, but you cannot feel pain," said the incredible agent, keeping instep and close to her commander.

"Incredible," he said with a smile, he turned his head slightly to look at her, in utter adoration.

"Like you are... agent Sophia," said commander Rico, resisting the burning urge to kiss her brilliant head.

"The team's position is right ahead sir," she said, gesturing towards the flashing spider drone, marking the rooms position.

"Mind the debris sir, it's the janitor's day off," she joked, squeezing the commander's muscular obliques with her trembling hand. She ran a single finger, over his rock-hard intercostal muscles, in a brief and daring, secret caress.

Sophia bit her lip to supress her desire, for the handsome commander and pressed on, over the littered tunnel floor, towards the rest of her team. She put her feelings aside and stepped into the secret room, still clutching Rico around his waist.

"Officer in the room" declared agent O'Hara, snapping to salute the commander.

Agent Sharky, likewise snapped her hand to salute him.

"Welcome back commander," said Sharky, smiling from behind her visor.

The 'click' of metal on stone, echoed around the large cold room, as commander Rico stepped into the chamber, with agent Sophia at his side.

"Thank you Sharky, it's good to be back," said Rico, activating his own respirator. He turned gingerly to agent Sophia.

"Thanks to you guys," he said to the team in general, but his eyes were fixed on her.

Sophia smiled deeply from behind the dark, protective plexi glass, of her protective visor. Commander Rico turned his attention back to Sharky.

"What do I need to see, so urgently sister?" asked Rico.

"Hold on to your hat sir and check this out," said the gigantic, agent O'Hara, advancing towards a group of large statues, arranged along one wall, inside individual alcoves.

Each one surrounded by ancient Mayan hieroglyphs and incredibly, intricate dioramas of warfare and prophecy.

Sophia called all the remaining drones to her position with a single thought, through her head dress third eye. Nine drones quickly appeared in the chamber, instantly positioning themselves on the wall and ceiling, in spider drone mode.

The drones shone bright, overlapping light, illuminating the life size statues and the ornate hieroglyphs, surrounding them.

"I mean... is this for real?" asked the astonished agent O'Hara, to the team at large.

Without saying a word, commander Rico approached the first statue.

A huge armoured goddess, holding a flat hollow disk Rico traced over the Deity with his torch, but stopped at the face.

He gasped, as the hairs on his neck stood on end, he marched from one end of the wall, to the other, fervently studying the exquisite statue, so life like and haunting. So hypnotised, that he could barely move, stunned by their majesty and likeness.

"They are us, aren't they? I mean they don't just look like us, they are us, aren't they ...sir?" asked agent O'Hara, her voice a little startled sounding.

A lesser human would be freaked out by the discovery, but O'Hara has never been a lesser anything.

San Diablo, the devils haven.

CHAPTER 20.

The hum of the hover boards thumped down the endless corridor, like a Herold announcing his knight's arrival.

The approaching end of the corridor was packed with vicious looking guards and their inmate deputies. The agents came closer and closer to the men, heading straight towards the gaggle of plebs. The guards became uneasy with this game of chicken and flinched hard in a recoil, as the agents came to a sudden stop, a mere fraction of an inch Infront of them.

The nearest guard unfolded himself embarrassedly, from his coward's squat and stood up straight again, glaring at the tall agent in front of him.

The mechanical looking agent smiled and lent slowly in towards the man's contorted face, he could feel the burn of embarrassment, from the man's shaking visage.

"Pussy," said the tall agent and laughed hard, in the livid officer's face.

The door to the little corridor was wide open, as was the thick oak door, adjoining the balcony to the warden's office.

The enraged guard looked down, as special agent Malone and his team, marched passed him into the short corridor.

Malone could feel the hate from the man and he liked it. The entire prison staff, were obsessed with him and not with what he was doing. All he had to do, was piss off as many of the warden's men as he possibly could and his actions would become invisible, hidden from sight, in a mist of hate and anger.

Malone turned to address the swell of angry men, circling in behind him from the corridor. He looked through the crowd, searching for his mark and bingo. His sunglasses had highlighted, one of the inmate deputies.

Malone pointed at the man, with a wagging finger.

"You, don't I recognise you?" asked Malone, in a very predatory tone.

The man, puzzled, pointed at himself in response.

"Nah man, I don't know you Gringo!" Spat the inmate, to the laughter of some of the others.

"Yes, it's little Carlos... Maria Jozas son?" continued Malone, laughing slightly.

"Ci," replied the man, confused, "How do you know mi Mamma?" he asked, a little elated at the memory of his dear Momma.

"When your father Philippe, was serving his time in San Quentin prison, me and my hommies would go round and fuck that fat, spick bitch, all night long." roared the agent, while making hip thrusts and spanking an imaginary sex partner.

The silence was electric, armed men, hesitant and uncertain, looked to each other in disbelief. One young guard stood frozen, with his mouth agape, vacantly staring at Malone and then to the furious, ex cartel enforcer, his teeth were bared in utter rage and the whites of his eyes, huge in his veiny head. The guard looked back again at agent Malone.

The veteran agent winked at the man and blew him a kiss.

The huge posse of deputies instantly exploded, into a storm of collective vengeance; the guards struggled desperately to keep the inmate deputy, from attacking the CIA agents.

The fray soon became a battle, between deputies and officers. Inmates and guards alike, began smashing each other with fist and by stick.

Right in the centre of the battle, the three agents stepped into the warden's corridor, closing the door behind them gently.

Agent Jeffries shrugged.

"Tough crowd tonight," he joked, without smiling, or missing a step, with Stirling and Malone.

The three agents approached the open doorway, into the warden's office. The warden was sat in his trophy chair, glaring straight daggers, at the three CIA men. Malone knocked three times on the door anyway.

"Come" shouted the warden, in an attempt to keep the upper hand, with the slippery, special agent. Malone and his team entered the large office, and slammed the door behind them, drowning out the noise of the guards, scuffling with their inmate deputies.

Behind the large mahogany desk, sat the disgusting warden, the huge Mr Black stood to the right and to the left, a small, but intense, elderly Japanese man, dressed in an expensive looking white suit, set against a deep burgundy, open shirt.

His open posture was relaxed but incredibly aggressive. The tranquil intensity of the man, held the agent's awareness, like a tiger, loose in the room.

"Come on in boys, don't be shy," bellowed the warden to the special agents, trying not to smirk at them.

Malone sensed a change in the warden's demeanour, like a veteran gambler, hiding a winning hand.

Malone turned his attention, back to the warden.

"Thus far warden, you have failed in your obligation to find one little prisoner and you impede us in our attempts, now tell us what you know! You, fat sack of shit!" said Malone, leaning over the desk aggressively.

Agent Jeffries of course, scanned the papers on the desk, exposed by Malones little display.

The warden, taken back by the audacity of the veteran spy, began clapping his filthy hands together in slow, mock applause.

"Well, well, well, very impressive agent Malone or should I say, double agent Malone? Yes, we know about that too, you smug, smooth, lanky assed, gaunt looking, son of a bitch.

What have you done to find the bastard, huh, sweet diddly squat! Now back up cowboy," said the warden, shooing the agent away with his hands.

Mr Black rolled up his sleeves, making a subtle display of hostility. The smart old gentleman, acknowledging the cue from Black, raised an eyebrow in acknowledgment, and widened his stance.

"Doctor Sakamura, I presume," said the vigilant agent Stirling.

The doctor tilted his head slightly, to look face on at the staunch special agent.

"Hhmm, who else?" replied Sakamura.

His voice like gravel, rough and cold, only added to the enigmatic energy, surrounding the last, real modern Samurai great one, or daimyo. The enigmatic older, turned his attention back to the warden and to Mr Black.

Commander Rico stood back in disbelief from the statues. He stepped closer, to re-examine one of the female statues, the light array from his helmet, illuminated the face, of the fierce looking soldier.

He gasped in realisation at what he saw, the statue was the exact likeness of agent Sophia, every detail identical, even down to her psych crown invention. Commander Rico kissed his knuckles and touched his forehead, then stomach, right breast then left, over his heart. The sign of the cross.

"It is us, no doubt about it, team Alpha?" said commander Rico, stiffening his posture and regaining his stoic warrior resolve.

"Ah hooo!" responded team Alpha, fully pumped from the return of their commander.

"We need to study this entire room and piece together what is expected of us. You all know me, and you know I don't buy into that fate crap, but I know that this statue is me and these ones, are you, so we can quit any debate. There's a reason we are here and we need to figure all this shit out! We Savvy?" asked the commander, rallying his team for a long and predestined mission.

"Eye sir," replied team Alpha, as one single unit. "Sophia, I want you to look for reoccurring shapes, patterns and symbols. O'Hara, I want you on these battle scenes, see what you make of them. Sharky, I need you checking every detail on the statues. Look for anything out of place, any clues. I'm gonna get to grips with the new upgrade," said commander Rico, gently patting the metal thigh muscles of his prosthetic leg, with the flat of his hand.

The incredible agent Sophia began fervently scanning over the ornate, Mayan Hieroglyphs. Three drones joined her in her task, slowly scanning the entire room.

Overlapping images, flickered, and highlighted with a flash of green. Sophia watched on, as image after image, flashed and stored over the smart screen, on her vambrace.

Agent O'Hara took a step back to take in the full scene displayed in the diorama, above the gigantic statue of herself.

Looking at the scene of combat, O'Hara felt the strangest pang of de Ja vu, like she could almost remember the stone being carved, by master artisans, from a far, bygone age.

One of agent Sophia's drones buzzed around the hulking agent, gathering data at the request of O'Hara herself. The drone documented the scenes, for a later presentation.

"Sir, the writing changes here," said Sophia, somewhat excited.

"This is a much older language than the hieroglyphs we've seen thus far and it's a linguistical system I've seen before," continued agent Sophia.

"What language?" asked Sharky, not looking up from studying the statue, of commander Rico.

"Ancient Sanskrit, the written word of the Indus valley civilisation. I'm absolutely certain I can translate the hieroglyphs. This wall is the key." said Sophia, with renewed vigour and confidence.

"How long?" asked Rico, impressed.

"As fast as I can sir. I'm overlapping the data from the drone, with the translations on this wall, to get a full translation to English, with the drones. Then I can upgrade one of them, to be the translator. Sending data and voice notes in real time, to decipher this entire language structure and enlighten us from the past," continued the genius agent, buzzing with purpose.

"That's incredible... make it happen," ordered the war-torn commander.

Rico began pacing the large stone room, getting faster and faster, as he came to a full sprint. He came to a halt at the far wall, Infront of a diorama of himself hanging from the stone chamber ceiling. He stared at the carved stone scene for a moment, then down, at the raptor like claws at the end of his foot.

The veteran commander, tapped the claws on the ground and looked up, thinking deeply. Suddenly a thought washed over him and he turned his attention, to a patch of low ceiling, bulged by the eons. With a deep breath and with great tenacity, he went for it.

Rico jumped off from the robotic leg and kicked out and over with the other. Rolling, the commander tucked into a back flip, pressing his momentum up, in a well-timed flurry of energy, the commander accelerated, feet first, towards the bulging chamber ceiling.

Commander Rico gripped hard, with the sharp claws of the prosthetic limb; and the metal talons pierced deep, into the cold rock face.

Rico stayed there for a moment, hanging from the ceiling like a bat asleep in a cave. Just like the ornate rock carving, he had seen only a minute prior. He let go with his claws and rolled his knees under himself, landing perfectly and near silently, on the cold, dusty stone floor of the hidden room.

"Now that, will come in handy," the commander said to himself nodding.

He looked back over to Sophia and smiled, standing for a moment, just in admiration of her, he longed for her more with every breath. There was a hole in him, an emptiness that only she could fill and he could love no other, but her. He loathed himself for never being courageous enough, to tell her how deeply he felt for her, or how beautiful she was to him, but better he felt, to find satisfaction in the presence of his love, than to scare it away, with heavy words of love.

He wiped the dust aggressively from his face. and his fingers lingered, on the large scars, Kris crossing his face. He closed his eyes and sighed deeply, into the empty space of the room, Rico straightened up and snapped out of his heart-breaking daydream.

Sophia, O'Hara and Sharky huddled together, to cross reference each other's findings, overlapping hypothesis and preparing a cohesive, but condensed presentation brief for their commander. The team shared their data, and after much deliberating, enlightened one another to the root translation, of that room of riddles.

Commander Rico pulled a leather Tabacco pouch, from his utility belt and rolled a cigarette, he needed a minute, for a smoke and a think.

He lent back against the wall and let his mind become blank and calm. Taking a drag of his cigarette, he blew the smoke out into the room. Tuning everything out, except the events that led him there.

A cold British voice, whispered, from deep within himself.

"The Rudra." Spoke the emptiness of the void.

Rico's eyes snapped open, it was all connected to the one man they were pursuing, the real reason they were detailed to Malone, they were there because of Him. They were caught up in a karmic web of events, all spun by him, the Rudra.

The commanders neck hair stood on end, at how deeply entwined in fate they all were. He felt the weight of it all on his shoulders and smiled, he embraced the challenge of it all.

He felt it on his shoulders and grinned, 'if not them, then who? Who else could fulfil such a challenge? Who else could stop the Hell on Earth? Who else, but team Alpha. HOO RAAH!

Commander Rico stretched his neck from side to side, it clicked and cracked, as tension was released from the rugged commanders, thick, muscular neck.

"Agent Sophia, how close are we to presentation?" asked Rico, now walking towards the huddled agents.

"Almost commander," replied Sophia, hurriedly uploading their findings, to one of the spider drones, open on the table.

Sophia's vambrace flickered as file after file, uploaded from the smart screen to the drone, then flashed green, indicating the completion of the upload.

The incredible agent, walked to the centre of the room, holding the drone like a baby in her arm. She kissed the drone and released it gently, into the room like a dove.

The robotic drone hovered in the centre of the secret chamber. Its rotary blades hummed quietly, punctuating the intense silence, of the ancient structure.

A single beam of brilliant blue light, shot out of the front of the drone, landing as a small blue dot, on the secret wall opposite.

The dot became bigger and spread over the first scene, spreading to the surrounding hieroglyphs. The blue light danced over the carvings, like the reflection of water, in the full moon light.

"This relief, being the first of the series, depicts the invasion and enslavement of the local Indigenous people, by a society known as the 'Jungle Lords' or 'Leopard people', as they are also referred as," said a smooth, synthetic, male voice, emanating from the drone.

"The Jungle Lords, left their home, deep in the Jungle of south America, following celestial movements, predicted by their astrological calendar, an area of the wall became highlighted in red light, revealing a familiar artefact.

"Is that the Mayan calendar, Alfred?" Sophia asked the drone.

"yes" replied Alfred, the interactive AI system of the drone.

"The 2012 calendar?" asked commander Rico, rubbing his eyes, as if he was imagining the surreal experience.

"No, that calendar ran out in 2012, this is the calendar prior to that," answered the robotic voice of Alfred.

"This calendar model, was made to keep track of an event of great evil. Every 56,000 earth years, or solar cycles, is the equivalent of one cycle, of deeper celestial events.

Galaxies, stars and planets, all cycle round each other, in an intricate dance, of the cosmic, physical forces. In particular, gravity.

The Jungle Lords tracked and recorded, the astrological movement of time, to predict a weakening of forces, between the underworld of demons and the world you know as home," continued the drone.

"The hell gate?" asked O'Hara, as if remembering a dream.

"Yes, agent O'Hara, the hell gate, an area of interdimensional space, co-inhabited at one small point, by two separate dimensional realities. The reality of Earth and the reality of Hell, co-exist at the same time and space, but are separate by physical, dimensional barriers.

At the point of one full cycle, of the Jungle Lords calendar, this point of contact, becomes much, much stronger, as conspiring celestial movement and incredible opposing gravitational forces, weaken the barrier. Thinning the membrane between the two dimensions," continued Alfred to the room.

"Alfred, how did the ancients find the Hell gate and why did they come, what was the payoff for them?" asked commander Rico, to the artificial personality.

"The warp energy, is immeasurably condensed and amplified at the mouth of the Hell gate, it can grant incredible power and ability to those with knowledge and instruction," replied Alfred.

"Alfred, how did they know to come here?" repeated commander Rico.

"As is human tradition commander, they followed a star. The Jungle Lords were advanced in mathematics and astrology, they followed the night sky religiously and predicted exactly, where the Hell gate would be.

The Indigenous slave race, speak of a single demonic entity, void of form that came through the Hell gate, many eons before the Jungle Lords, drifting through the dark, as a phantom.

Finally, the entity or high dragon, as it is described here," a red light, outlined a carving of a huge dragon, descending on a bound captive.

Another red laser, highlighted another block of hieroglyphs, above the exquisitely, detailed scene.

"Entered into a bound, prisoner of war, a captured enemy soldier. To take temporary residence, in the body of the unfortunate man.

Taking over full control of the man. Guiding and advising the king, on matters of conquest and war. In a span of only five years, the Jungle people rose in power and wealth, dominating the entire region," said the robotic voice of the drone, moving the blue outline further along the wall, to the final scene of the first wall, in the secret stone chamber.

"The possessed inmate however, could not endure the agony of the warp for long. The fragile human structure, simply comes apart, atom by atom, until nothing.

The dragon, formally referenced to as 'Baal-Zib-bub, instructed the Mages and the king, to find a warrior of great strength, an indominable brute of a man, as shown here," said Alfred, highlighting a relief carving, of an enormous and dominating Mayan warrior.

The kings own body guard, in full Mayan armour, dressed as a Jaguar. Holding an enormous bludgeon in one hand and the severed head of a rival enemy soldier in the other.

"The soldier lay voluntarily on the sacrificial alter, willingly accepting the demonic entity, into himself and knowingly dammed himself to hell.

The scribe speaks of the man's own soul being ripped from his heart and cast into the eternal agony of the warp. thrown aside like garbage, to make way for the demonic Baal-Zib-Bub.

The entity demanded human blood to sustain itself in this dimension and in that body. The blood came by the gallon, in the form of still beating, human hearts, cut from the chest of terrified, human prisoners.

It was he, commander, who taught the Jungle Lords, how to harness the warp, map the heavens and build precise pyramids. The fame and success of the Jungle Lords, increased and so did their desire for total dominion.

Blinded by power, they set off on foot, over many years of conquest, until they came here, commander." Said the AI Alfred.

The drone turned at ninety degrees and again, the single blue dot, covered the next wall of the series and the next set of hieroglyphs and mysterious symbols.

"Alfred, what about the Sanskrit inscriptions?" asked O'Hara, slightly puzzled.

"What about them agent O'Hara? You'll have to be more specific," replied Alfred, smartly.

"How is it, that we find a language from the Indus Vally, here, in an ancient Mayan pyramid, in North America?" Continued the intimidating agent O'Hara.

"Sanskrit, is the language of the Indigenous people taken as slaves," answered Alfred.

"How is that even possible?" blurted O'Hara, almost doubting the AI.

"The far ancient society, of the Indus Vally, had their age of conquest too, agent. The data collected here." The deep red laser, outlined a section of the Sanskrit text and recurring symbols, dotted around the chamber.

"All describe a time before the separation of the continents, when all the land of the Earth, was one super continent, Pangea, as it is known in modern times. It was once called Kosala to its ancient inhabitants, some one Billion plus years ago," continued Alfred, outlining with the red laser, the first diorama of the wall.

A large carved scene depicting a series of pyramids forming a large pentagon, surrounding three solid pentagon, temple buildings. With a large, bloated looking dragon devouring bound captives.

The scene was surrounded by dragons, descending, as it were, to the earth.

San Diablo, the devils haven.

CHAPTER 21.

The warden laughed and shook his head, his bloated, swollen shoulders, bounced up and down, jiggling his many chins and wobbling his pale, sweaty jowls. He stood up from his Rino skin chair and walked slowly behind Mr Black and Doctor Sakamura.

Silently, the warden gazed out of the large viewing window, for several minutes. The three agents silently stood; attention fixed on the warden's men.

"You know something Mr fancy Britches?" said the warden, interrupting the silence.

"A thought occurs. This whole place, this entire facility does not even exist... officially." said the warden, reciting a pre- rehearsed speech.

"That's correct, Mr Scruffy britches," said special agent Malone, returning fire to the warden and deliberately, interrupted the man.

"What about it?" grunted special agent Stirling, not taking his eyes off the enigmatic, Doctor Sakamura.

"Be patient sweetheart, I'm getting there," said the warden, in a grotesque, sexual voice.

The warden turned from the window, to face the room once again.

"And you boys, you don't officially exist either. Officially, you were never here. Isn't that so, you, smug bastard?" the warden enquired, savagely.

"Well, nothing gets by you, does it? apart from the salad bowl, that is'" added special agent Jeffries, sarcastically.

"Perhaps a cleanse might help," mocked Malone.

"He needs fucking cleansing, the d.i.r.t.y bastard," added Stirling, sensing Malone's plan to fluster the beastly man.

"I've had turds that smell better," said agent Jeffries, jumping in and backing up his brother agents.

"And me!" continued the warden, trying not to show any anger.

"Get to the point," heckled special agent Malone, laughing.

"There's nothing pointy on him sir, he's totally round, like a balloon filled with custard," added Jeffries, pouring more fuel, to the warden's fire, denying him the impact he was hoping for.

 Interrupting and mocking the warden, was now the agents only task. Get him to make a mistake, make the awful man reveal his hand too soon, to the advantage of Americas finest agents.

"And none of the inmates, even exist..." began the warden again, now shaking visibly, with anger.

"BAAHHH... on with it fatty," barked special agent Stirling, interrupting the warden once again.

The warden, totally enraged, leapt out of his chair and slammed the desk top, with much more force than he had ever displayed prior.

"YOU, ARSEHOLE, FUCKING GET SOME!!!"

Shouted the short, stout, but furious warden.

"Sakamura San, hit it," demanded the warden, turning his bright red face, to the Samurai.

The enigmatic gentleman, raised a single eyebrow in disgust at the warden, for addressing him so, then, with a nonchalant sigh, he pressed the face of his large, gold watch.

The mechanism within the timepiece clicked and the face of the watch, blinked to red.

The elder Samurai Lord, threw his arms out to his sides and lifted his chin upwards slightly. His focus locked all the time, onto the three agents, now removing their jackets, and weapons.

"As you are so few in number, I will not use my blades," said the Samurai mercifully.

Pieces of body armour flew from their hiding places, to the Doctor, at blinding speed. Armour clicked and twisted, as it quickly attached itself to Doctor Sakamura, the lord of war.

Not the usual body armour of the Samurai, but this Daimyo, was the modern embodiment of his proud, blood line dynasty. It was more like the swat style armour of the space marines, but in the style and function, of the Karuta-Gane armour, worn by his warrior Lord, ancestors.

The elderly man leapt effortlessly, over the warden and his desk. With a single front flip somersault, he cleared the distance, landing in front of the agents, in a heartbeat.

"Ready gentlemen?" asked the enigmatic Samurai earnestly.

"Almost Sir," replied special agent Malone placing his assault weapon on the floor and removing his sunglasses.

The three agents stood in front of the Samurai, in readiness and high alert.

"Great one, it is unfortunate you are attached to the warden and not us, I ask your leave to strike you," said special agent Stirling, placing his right fist against his open left hand and respectfully bowing, before the great Samurai Lord.

"Granted gentlemen, you have until the count of three," said Sakamura, graciously.

Mr Black stepped around the table, making his way towards the agents.

"Stay away please Mr Black, there are only three of them," asked the Samurai politely.

Malone attacked first, throwing a heavy hay maker, which the Samurai Lord dodged, as if the entire room had slowed down, but him. He moved quickly and effortlessly, like a ghost in the room.

The enigmatic Doctor gently placed his right hand behind his back, while side stepping away from a powerful front kick, from special agent Jeffries, while easily swatting away special agent Stirling's left jab, right cross, combination.

The Samurai Lord, stepped closer into the centre of the three agents, giving up his tactical advantage for the sake of fairness and honour. The way of Bushido, perfectly personified.

The three special agents, launched attack, after attack attempting to subdue the elder, but to no avail, the expert fists of the veteran agents, hit nothing but air. The Samurai moved around the men gracefully, but menacingly, as he swatted the attacks of the three men with his right hand behind his back, without even breaking a sweat, in the stifling office, nor even, was he out of breath.

The faceless special agents fought on, flurry after flurry of kicks and punches, harmlessly parried and dodged, by the experienced warrior.

Mr Black walked backwards, back to the side of the warden, hypnotised by the dazzling display of martial perfection.

The warden sat back in his high-backed chair, enjoying the fight, and visibly aroused, enjoying the humiliation of the agents.

"The contract was not for dancing! Mr Sakamura... beat the shit out of them! Now!" ordered the warden, disrespectfully.

Doctor Sakamura, nodded angrily at the warden.

"As you wish" spat Sakamura, venomously.

"As I command!" bellowed the warden, standing up from his chair.

With one single movement, the daimyo had landed a back fist to Stirling, blocking the agents own punch with a fast, snap of movement.

He delivered a side kick to Malone's hip, sending the special agent to the ground, Malone rolled with the energy of the attack, back to his feet and back into the fight.

Special agent Jeffries however, smiled a wry, predatory smile.

"King ten, hut, queen ten," barked the genius special agent Jeffries, to his battle brothers, Stirling and Malone.

Doctor Sakamura looked up, only for a moment, but long enough for agent Malone to grab hold of the Samurai's, large shoulder armour and wrap his legs around the front of the man. Hooking in around his legs, and anchoring in behind the thin armour plates, on his thighs and at the same time, agent Stirling snaked his legs around the great one's ankles, snapping into a figure four leg lock. Sending the three of them, into a knot of combat.

Agent Jeffries jammed his foot under the Samurai's hip armour and pulled up and back, with the great one's arm locked out straight, against the agent's knee.

Mr Black dashed to the aid of the downed Samurai, but the warden held up a hand, stopping the huge officer in his tracks.

"Be patient Mr Black," said the warden, transfixed on the ensuing combat.

Suddenly, special agent Jeffries flew across the room, slamming feet first against the wall. The agent distributed the force of the impact, by bending his knees deeply and side rolling, onto the floor. Dusting himself off, the agent dashed back into the fight.

The Samurai Doctor Sakamura, kicked out, sending agent Stirling rolling out of his figure four leg lock, sending the veteran agent, across the floor.

The Samurai elder twisted like a snake, out of agent Malone's grip and into a one-armed hand stand. Landing weightlessly, in a deep squat on the edge of the warden's desk.

The three special agents, regrouped at a respectful distance, from the personification of war itself, the venerable, Doctor Sakamura.

The three CIA men, dusted themselves off and clicked their necks in unison. They each placed the clenched fist of their right hands, into the flat palm of the left.

They extended their arms, out straight and then back to just Infront of their chests. A salutation of sorts, from one warrior, to a greater warrior. A mark of respect, to the superior martial artist, about to take their lives.

The Samurai slowly and effortlessly, placed one foot and then the other, onto the decadently carpeted floor.

He returned the gesture of salutation, back to his almost, worthy opponents.

"It is indeed a shame, that I am attached to your adversary and not you..." began the great Samurai.

"Yes, but the CIA don't have your ancestors' ashes though, do they? No, but I do! Now kick their asses... NOW!!!" interrupted the warden, rudely.

Special agent Stirling raised an eyebrow in anger, at the warden's audacity to the great one. Malone however, found the experience very interesting indeed, 'leverage', thought the veteran special agent.

"Nothing personal gentlemen," said the ominous Samurai, steadily advancing towards the three special agents, he crackled with intensity and menace, as he moved in for the kill.

San Diablo, the devils haven.

CHAPTER 22.

"We are damn deep in this shit huh commander?" agent Sharky asked Rico, wide eyed.

"Balls deep," sighed the commander.

"Just how I like it," flirted agent Sophia.

She blushed and turned her back slightly, in embarrassment.

Commander Rico laughed and patted her on the shoulder, his large hand, slid down to the small of her back, lingering momentarily, before removing it.

She trembled internally at his touch. How she ached for him, the object of her desire, her commander, her Rico.

"Alfred, store this image, it's a map of the entire area and keep an overlapping trace, of our position in relation to it," ordered the commander, to the spider drone guide.

"Of course, commander," replied the polite, robotic voice of Alfred.

"Yes, but where do we come into this?" asked agent Sharky, folding her arms, bored with the history lesson.

"This really will be much faster, without all the interruptions," chided Alfred.

"All good things to those who wait," said agent O'Hara gently.

The giant soldier, gently placed a huge hand across Sharkys shoulder. Agent Sharky closed her eyes blissfully at the tenderness of O'Hara's, touch and tone.

"The outer complex of pyramids," said Alfred smoothly, highlighting the array of pyramids, forming a pentagon around the outer temple building, with a red blinking outline. Showing thirty pyramids, forming a pentagon, six in a line, five lines in all to the agent.

"Energy generating in nature," said Alfred, continuing with haste.

"Energy?" what for?" Sophia asked the spider drone.

"The energy generated and maintained by the pyramids, keep the dimensional frequency conducive, to support the existence of the extra-dimensional entities, or the demonic inhabitants of Hell, as they are also known," answered Alfred, in a slightly smug, robotic voice.

"The volunteers, held in the outer temple complex," Alfred indicated with the flashing red Lazer, outlining the outer pentagon, on the carved stone scene.

"Became possessed willingly, by the formless dimensional interlopers, for one day.

In that time, the Deamons must murder, savagely and terribly, the captives imprisoned at the centre temple complex... the blood of the terrified inmates, is to be smeared over the centre temple, covering the entire complex with the sacrificial blood and suffering, of the condemned prisoners, bereft of a second chance. Thus, weakening the thin veil between Hell and Earth, allowing the king of the Deamons, 'Shay-ta-han' and his myriad legion, of Hell spawn demons, a window of opportunity, to break through the realities and conquer all life on Earth. Raising a second Hell on Earth and allowing them, a physical existence for all time, here," continued Alfred, to team Alpha.

The inmates held in the second Temple, were kept in a state of base emotional stasis," said Alfred, continuing his presentation brief.

"See! Now what... the fuck... does that even mean Alfred?" asked commander Rico, annoyed.

"All the base emotions, or sin as it is also known, rage, jealousy, lust... all the worst states of being, fear, loathing, all of them. The captives were made to suffer and, in that suffering, came the energy signature needed to attract the demonic entities to their devotees, in the outer temple," replied Alfred, smoothly.

"We are in the pyramid here," announced Alfred, highlighting the uppermost pyramid on the diorama, with the flashing red laser.

"What happened? I mean, Hell didn't come on Earth... did it?" enquired agent Sharky, perplexed.

"That ritual was the beginning step, towards that end goal," the red laser swept the wall.

Flickering red light, danced over the intricate hieroglyphs, all along the stone wall. Stopping sharply on a familiar image.

"The Mayan calendar!" exclaimed commander Rico.

"Correct commander, this entire area was swallowed up by the desert. The lush forest, became a desert over time, from the corruption of the Hell gate. In just one day, the power of the warp swept over this land, covering the pyramids and preserving the Hell gate... this calendar began on that day, a little over five thousand years ago," answered Alfred, the upgraded spider drone.

"But that ran out in twenty twelve, didn't it?" asked Sophia, puzzled.

"No, the Mayans, like their Indus Vally predecessors, used zero as the datum point in their mathematical equations. The architects of this calendar, were far more precise, than the Gregorian model used today. Also, the calendar is based on celestial events in elliptical orbits. They allowed for the stretching of orbital paths and overlapping solar and lunar eclipses as a stop, start trigger. Landing the completion of this model, at the next full moon." Alfred paused to consider his words.

That is when the conditions will be conducive and when Baal-Zib-Bub, will make his move. When the final calendar of the Maya, comes to an end and that of Hell may come to be," continued Alfred, moving the blue light over to the next wall and the next set of hieroglyphs. Carved it would seem, for the eyes of Ricos team Alpha and only to be seen right then, at the appointed time, by the appointed team.

"Hoo Rah!"

"Well, when IS the next full moon?" asked agent Sharky, urgently.

"In five days', time, dear," answered the impressive agent O'Hara, absent- mindedly.

"Correct, agent O'Hara," said Alfred, hovering quietly in the centre of the room.

"But mother Earth had a few tricks, up her sleeve too. The same soil that drank the blood of the ancients, gave birth to you, the four of you as shown here," said Alfred, indicating in red, four unique sets of hieroglyphs, showing seed, plant, moon, and sun.

"Four of the greatest spiritual adepts of the priest class, or brahmins, performed soul crushing, spiritual preparation, called sadhana for many years, leading up to the completion of the temple site.

On the night of the full moon alignment, the four masters, voluntarily left their own bodies into the ether, releasing their spirit or energy bodies. Sacrificing physical form and their very lives, to wait for the time to become right, and the conditions conducive, with astrological markers in the night sky.

One by one, they became you at the moment of conception. They sacrificed what remained of their energy into you, team Alpha.

They followed the stars to find you and give themselves to you, so you could become the extra ordinary human beings, you are today. A force fit for the task ahead and the trials, within this ancient place," continued Alfred the wonder drone, to the astonishment of his team.

"The ancients have left you weapons, tools and instructions," said Alfred, moving the blue highlight further across the wall, to the five statues stood in alcoves, at the centre of the wall.

"Who is this guy?" asked agent Sharky, pointing at the statue of a naked man in meditation.

"He is referenced to, only as 'The Rudra', he is the embodiment of God on Earth and the prophesised destroyer of the Hell gate, or..." he paused, "the world, the Rudra will not allow the Reighn of Hell on Earth. With a dance, it is said, he has the power to destroy even time," said Alfred, illuminating the statue of the man and surrounding hieroglyphs.

Commander Ricos body hair, stood on end in a moment of ecstatic, personal realisation.

"He's the escaped inmate, Malone sent us after, he was always going to be here and so were we, I think I've been hearing his voice since the cave in... that bastard Suarez, he is even a part of all this. well, you can't escape your fate, can you?" asked the commander, staring sideways, at the lovely agent Sophia.

"This is a big deal team, thank God we are the chosen ones and not some other assholes, we ARE team Alpha are we not? The very best there is," announced commander Rico, emotionally to his team.

"AAAH HOOO" roared team Alpha, in unison.

"What weapons Alfred?" Sophia asked the drone.

"Please step this way team," asked Alfred, indicating to sets of footprints Infront of the statues.

"Please stand Infront of your respective statue," asked Alfred politely.

The Samurai Lord, Doctor Sakamura, with the speed of a coiled cobra, launched his offensive on the three special agents.

As fast as thought itself, the incredible elder, had landed a hard right cross straight into the face, of special agent Malone. The large purple bruise, instantly appeared on the agent's cheek.

Special agent Stirling, dashed to the aid of the downed agent, only to have his leading leg, kicked from under him, followed by a stinging snap kick to the groin. The CIA man hit the ground vomiting, from the pain in his balls.

The staunch special agent, pulled his knees under him and with a phenomenal display of will, snapped back to his feet.

Malone, joined by Jeffries and Stirling, threw their all at the Samurai Lord, punches were parried and kicks were blocked, as the superior fighter, wove himself closer and closer, in the midst of the three agents.

Special agent Stirling summoned one final attack, punching fiercely at the great one, but the Samurai snaked his arm around and under the arm of the agent, holding the exhausted warrior in an arm lock. Jeffries came in immediately after, with a fierce left cross of his own. The Samurai, effortlessly intercepted the punch and with a twist of his wrist, the Samurai pulled Jeffries arm under and over, that of agent Stirling's, while taking a front kick to the face.

 The Samurai absorbed the force of the attack within his own body, grounding the energy harmlessly to the ground.

Agent Malone kicked again, but this time the attack landed in a narrow space between his entangled brother agents. The Samurai closed the gap, with the flick of his hip, snaring Malone and the others together.

All three men were held fast, pinned by one glorious hand of the great Samurai Lord.

"Break his fucking arm," shouted the warden, gurning with arousal, excited by the defeat of the agents, particularly that of special agent Malone.

The Samurai Daimyo raised his free arm, towards the ceiling, in preparation of attack.

The warden stood, licking his lips, almost unable to control himself, lost in a state of violent Exstacy. The vile man took a deep breath in, with anticipation of the Samurai's violence.

The warden's thick, heavy, office door, burst open. A livid, blood-spattered inmate deputy, entered the room and lifted his shot gun to the cradle of his shoulder, aiming it straight at the agents.

"You son of a bitch!" shouted the inmate, to special agent Malone.

In an instant, Doctor Sakamura reached into his immaculately styled hair, pulling out a long, thin, hair pin from his bound white locks and with a flick, threw it at the inmate, with such force, that it went straight through the Deputies skull, and embedded itself in the corridor wall.

The Samurai Lord, released the three agents and stepped back two spaces.

The bloodied, bruised and defeated agents, got to their feet and saluted the Great one, bowing deeply in respect and gratitude, even, through such great pain.

"Mr Black, what in fucks pretty name, is going on?" demanded the warden.

"Go! Sort this out," barked the warden, slapping Black on the rump, as he set off towards the door.

"And you, you, yellow bastard, you! When I say do, you fucking do, understand?" demanded the vile beast of a man, to the honourable Doctor Sakamura.

The great one said nothing and the warden was wise enough, not to push the matter.

"Black, what's happened?" demanded the warden, in a more genial tone.

j

San Diablo, the devils haven.

CHAPTER 23.

Team Alpha looked to each other and to commander Rico, for any sign of a command. That was the reputation that they had gained among their own circles, they silently moved as one as if they were psychically connected and could read the minds, and hearts, of each other.

When in reality, they knew each other's will to such an extent, that they were in many ways, one. The trust in their commander, was without question, and absolute. A war trained team, of super soldiers.

Then as one, they followed his lead and stepped across the room. Passing Alfred, Sophia kissed her finger and touched the drone on its side.

Rico stopped Infront of the stone footprints, immediately followed by his team.

"What's next Alfred?" asked the rugged commander, stoically.

"The hieroglyphs depict you all standing, on your respective footsteps, releasing the weapons you will need, to complete the mission, commander," answered Alfred, helpfully.

Team Alpha stepped forward as one. Nothing happened for a moment and then a 'click', happened. The sounds of heavy Coggs meshing together filled the room; then suddenly the floor under each agent, gave way. Sending team Alpha down through the ground, in some dark, stone, tunnel.

"ALFRED!" screamed agent Sophia, reaching up. The spider drone flew over to the spot, as the floor re-appeared, sealing them inside.

"Good buy commander," said Alfred hovering in the silence. Alfred retreated back, to the centre of the room and began re-scanning, once again.

Three of the remaining spider drones flew over to him, the four drones began flashing lights at each other, communicating in binary code. The flickering lights made the shadows dance and move and fight, in the silent, secret chamber.

Alfred and the three spider drones, flew into position above the stone footprints, positioned Infront of the four

statues of the warriors. Alfred of course, hovered above
Sophia's statues footprint.

The floor beneath them, flickered for a moment and then
disappeared completely, exposing four open shafts
leading down. Curving off view in a long arc, of stone
and darkness.

The four drones hovered for a brief moment, before
rapidly descending, into the small dark tunnels. Minutes
later and after much spiralling and descending through
the pyramid itself, the drones emerged together, in a
long, tall room. The walls angled inwards, forming an
equilateral triangle with the floor.

"Alfred?" came the voice of agent O'Hara, her booming
voice echoed deeply in the chamber, reverberating and
bouncing, from one smooth quart's wall, to the other.

 The whole room buzzed, with a tangible, electric
energy, like pylons around a power station.

"Alfred... what the fuck, is going on?" Asked
commander Rico, from the darkness of the room.

"Hello again commander," said Alfred. The four drones-
initiated luminance mode, illuminating the plexi plastic
exoskeleton, of their outer shells.

The room lit up brightly, as the light from the drones, became amplified many times over, by the smooth, mirror like quartz walls. The drones zipped across the room, to the position of commander Rico and team Alpha.

The other drones fanned out and hovered Infront of the long wall. Small beams of light, shot out from them, projecting on the opposite wall a map of the complex, indicating with a flashing red dot, their current position.

"Your weapons training begins here commander, the exit is sealed in. You will either pass the test and leave, or fail and remain in this tomb for ever," replied the drone, flatly.

The drones projected a series of images and hieroglyphs on the stone wall, giving a snap presentation of the situation, as it evolved.

"In the corners of the room you will find a flat, smooth handprint, the text instructs you to please, place your right hand onto it. This is the first test," continued Alfred, facing the team.

"Pahh, I don't like all this temple of doom, Indianna Jones bullshit sir, not one bit," spat agent Sharky, indignantly.

"I hear you sister, but we have no choice. We must play the pyramids game, or we are going to be trapped in this room for ever! fuck that! Come team, let's do this!" answered commander Rico, rallying his weary team.

"Eye sir... Hoo Raah!" confirmed the steely agent Sharky, always full of fight.

Commander Rico walked towards, one of the four, stone plaques.

"Fan out team, one each," he said to his stalwart team of agents.

Sophia, O'Hara and Sharky, separated off to each corner, finding the hand print plaques, straight away.

"You must keep your hand firmly on the print, flat... and also, it said you must fearlessly hold your hand, for five minutes no matter what, or this room will close in and slowly crush us all. It is a test of courage," said Alfred, encouragingly.

"Are we courageous team?" barked the stoic commander Rico.

"Aah hooo," replied the team aggressively. Rico smiled with pride.

"Hoo Raah," he continued, putting his hand flat against the stone, palm print, In front of him. He looked to the rest of the team, at their respective corners of the room, doing the same.

Rico took a deep breath and filled his broad chest, with the cool air of the room, waiting for the pyramids next deadly test.

A quiet, low hissing noise could be herd as enthobotanical herbs and their compounds, reacted with ancient liquids. The reactive alkaline compounds from the peyote cactus, mescaline, released from their ancient containers, after many centuries of containment, by the pyramids many mechanisms. All triggered by the handprint plaques, now compressed by team Alpha.

Gas immediately formed in the chamber and a heavy odorous gas, saturated with hallucinogens, began invisibly, rolling down the smooth quart's walls of the chamber, down towards the commander and his team.

"Hallucinogenic compounds detected, keep your minds strong and keep your hands on the prints. Pick a spot in front of you and keep your hands steady, good luck team Alpha," said Alfred, earnestly.

The hallucinogenic gas, hit commander Rico like a ton of bricks, the gas entered his lungs and immediately, entered his blood stream. His knees buckled slightly as his mind bent, sending him deeply, into a waking nightmare.

He closed his eyes and breathed deeply for a moment, mustering his courage, holding desperately on to a rapidly warping mind.

"HOLD FIRM TEAM, REMEMBER... THE... Custard," said the steely commander, melting into the mind-bending, psychedelic trip.

He opened his eyes, only to witness his hand not on the wall, but in a raging fire. The pain was excruciating, but he watched on with a face like stone as the flesh, burned on his hand. The foul smell of burning human flesh, filled his nose and throat. Every instinct in him, screamed at him to snatch his hand from the flame, an ordinary man would have, but then a normal man, would not command team Alpha.

Rico smiled and silently thanked God, that he was not an ordinary man. After all, an ordinary man, would never meet her. The idea of her drove him on, she inspired him to greater possibilities, she made him extraordinary, and that gave him his fire, the fire of a commander.

The flames abated and the pain disappeared, the flesh healed on his badly burned hand, before his unreliable eyes.

"Firm team, hold the wall, bdrrale..." mumbled the commander, staring fiercely at his hand on the smooth stone wall, his mind fully gripped, by the trip.

Water began bubbling up beneath the cold stone floor, slowly filling the room. It felt icy cold against the leg of commander Rico. Slowly rising higher and higher.

Rico could feel it pouring into his boot, as it rose higher up to his crotch. The freezing water was so painful, it felt like fire, against his saturated skin.

The icy water, rose up to his nose and still, the stout commander Rico, held firm his resolve. Bending both logic and instinct to his will, he kept his hand on the wall, even as the water rose above him.

Rico could hold his breath no longer, but he would not be the one to blink first, eventually, the room relented and the water disappeared, leaving the commander, dry again and gasping for air.

There was a loud click, from behind the agent's hands, as the timed, pressure pad mechanisms, locked into place, releasing the antidote, into the room.

Agent Sophia breathed deeply, inhaling the vaporised anti psychedelic.

The nightmare world vanished, returning her at last, to the present, firm reality.

She looked around the room, to the rest of the team, all standing firm, all had done their part.

"Team Alpha, sound off," ordered commander Rico.

"Sophia, ready,"

"Sharky, ready,"

"O'Hara, ready,"

"Rico, ready,"

Team Alpha responded with pride, they had all passed that test, of the ancients.

"You can have your hands back now, well done team Alpha," said Alfred, to the room.

They moved their hands away from the wall and stood back from it, gravitating to one another instinctively.

"Now what Alfred?" asked the commander.

A loud snap, echoed loudly around the room, as a large part of the middle wall, sank slowly into the ground.

"Well, I guess we go this way, commander," said Alfred, smugly.

Alfred and the other drones, zipped through the door way and into a new, but familiar room.

"All clear sir," said agent Sophia, looking up from her vambrace screen.

 The commander chopped the air with his hand and arm out straight, pointing into the darkness of the secret entrance.

"Team Alpha, move out! "Ordered Rico, leading the advance.

San Diablo, the devils haven.

CHAPTER 24.

"Mr Black!" Roared the ever-impatient warden.

"Black!!!" repeated the angry little man.

The thick oak door burst open, from the sheer force of Mr Black flying through it, landing through a backwards roll on the thick, shag pile carpet, in the warden's office.

A man stepped through the door way, totally naked and holding a large, ornate wooden box. The man's eyes burned with such intensity, that they seemed to hide his face, as if veiling him, in shadow and in light.

The room buzzed with silence, adding to the quiet menace, of the naked man.

The warden, CIA agents and the semi-conscious Mr Black, were spellbound, transfixed on his face and his incredible presence, but not Doctor Sakamura, he was focused only, on what the stranger was carrying.

"Doctor Sakamura San, please accept this token," said the man, in a respectful tone, through a dry, British accent.

The Samurai took the ancient box from him. He held the box tight to his chest and closed his eyes, as he connected himself, once again, with the ashes of his forebears.

"Mr Warden, I would like to leave your employ now," said the great one, walking towards the bruised special agent. He bowed slightly and shook special agent

Malone's hand, secretly placing something in his hand, something useful.

"It would be nice to drink tea with you, if next we meet, instead of fighting. I hope you understand," warned Doctor Sakamura, politely.

"There is still more blood for you to bathe in, before you are clean, good doctor," said the naked man, to the Samurai Lord.

"Yes, lots of blood, but not here, not for him, and certainly not for you," replied the Samurai bluntly, eyeballing the man.

"You have not aged a day... Kaiju," whispered the Samurai intensely, into the naked man's face, and just walked out the door, not looking back, the human God of war left the room, leaving naught, but bruises and confusion in his wake.

So, what does a man have to do to get a cup of tea around here?" Asked the man, grinning like a Cheshire cat.

"You... You... You, cost me my slave, oh boy your gonna pay for that," stammered the warden, fit to burst.

He slammed a hidden button, on the front of the desk. Instantly wooden panels slid away and four teams, of heavily armed and armoured elite guards, swarmed into the room. The Lazer scopes of myriad assault weapons, dotted all over the man's naked body, like a deadly rash.

The naked man looked down at the multitude of red dots on his chest, then looked back up at the audacious guards, and laughed.

"By all means chaps! Keep them pointed, if it makes you feel better. Ah, agent Malone, don't you think it's a little odd, that you haven't heard from the search party. I only pray, that Rico finds what he's looking for," said the man, smoothly.

"Rudra?" asked special agent Malone, squinting through swollen eyes.

"Don't just stand there you spineless fuck weasel, arrest him!" Barked the warden, dragging the enormous Mr Black, back to his feet.

Mr Black shook his head, trying to focus like a drunk, trying to will himself sober.

"Rudra! Warden, we need to interview this man," said special agent Malone, urgently.

"You've got some bastard nerve Malone., ARREST HIM, get that inmate in chains now!" said the warden, pushing the monster Mr Black, towards the Rudra.

The armed prison guards slowly, advanced on the Rudra, guns pointed at the naked man.

"Hands behind your back, palms towards each other," growled Mr Black, reaching for the snap cuffs at his hip.

"Well, seeing as you asked so nicely," said the Rudra cheerfully, he placed his hands behind his back in compliance.

"I was starting to get bored, waiting for you to find me," said the naked man, sarcastically.

"How did you get that urn?" asked the warden.

"You can fuck right off mate!" Retorted the Rudra, angrily.

His sophisticated accent absent and replaced with a gruff Cockney one, angry, vicious, cockney one.

Mr Black snapped the titanium cuffs, hard against the Rudra's wrists.

"Nice and secure Mr Black, just like Bosnia is. Wouldn't you agree?" Mocked the Rudra, in a sickly-sweet tone.

Knowing exactly what buttons to press, with the big man.

Mr Black spun the naked inmate, around violently and slammed his forehead, hard into the Rudra's laughing mouth. The head-butt connected, with a sickening crunch.

Mr Black staggered backwards, in a daze. Malone noted a trickle of blood, running out of the large brute's ear. Black took another step backwards, away from the Rudra and with a final gasp of air, dropped dead on the warden's floor.

"Oh dear, silly Mr Black," said the Rudra, in a horribly fake voice of concern.

"Mr White! You're up," sighed the warden, casually waving a podgy, limp wrist, towards a hulking, African officer. The tall and densely muscular officer, stepped forward mechanically.

Agent Malone could tell by the tribal scarring, of the man's face and hands, that this was an outlaw king, a decorated slayer of men.

The agents noted various implants and surgical upgrades, jutting from his neck and head. One of the professor's godless creations, a mechanically re-animated, dead man. A soul unable to leave its prison tomb, trapped and controlled by the professor's implants.

Enhanced and improved by the various augmentations, the dead prisoner became a slave to the darkness, and a toy played with, at the whim of demons.

The hulking Mr White stood forward and gave a sharp salute to the warden, then bound towards the hand cuffed man, purposefully. With a huge swing, the enslaved soul Mr White, with all his force, arced a heavy punch into the abdomen of the shackled Rudra.

Nothing. The naked inmate didn't even blink, he just stood there, staring down at the angry, ball of disgustingness, the warden.

The Rudra turned his attention, from the warden back to the three special agents, now fully suited and booted, sunglasses on and firearms back in their holsters.

"You were wise to retain Rico in your service agent Malone. I do so look forward to meeting him... Well, in the flesh I mean," said the Rudra, addressing Malone in particularly.

"Nice to see you've moved with the times Baal," he continued, snapping his attention back to the warden.

"Very you," added the Rudra, looking round the room, with disdain.

"Tacky and decadent," mocked the Rudra, laughing at the warden.

"Mr White, hit him again," ordered the raging warden, fit to burst.

BANG, BANG, BANG, Mr White delivered a right, left, right, body shot combination, savagely into the prisoner's rib cage. The big man stopped punching and stared into the eyes of the bound inmate.

"Pillock," said the Rudra dryly, mocking the abomination.

Mr White growled and began a flurry, of furious attacks. He punched, kicked, elbowed, kneed and chopped, all in a savage minute and a half, of wanton violence.

Mr White eventually stopped his attack, panting and exhausted, holding onto the captive man for stability. He looked again in disbelief, at the naked inmate, not a mark on him, not a scratch.

The Rudra looked back at the panting Mr White, with utter disgust.

"If you had shown that effort to your young wife, she wouldn't have slept with your brother. Food for thought old chap," giggled the Rudra, mocking the memory of the augmented Mr White, motionless and vacant in his fury.

The Rudra laughed loudly.

"He's blown a gasket!" He said laughing maniacally.

"You may take me to my residence now," said the Rudra, to the recovering Mr White.

"Take him to the hole for now, I'll deal with this bastard myself," said the warden.

He turned to face the handcuffed Rudra.

"Once I've taught him some, God damned manners!" Threatened the warden, through tightly clenched teeth.

"You can't teach me, fuck all mate," spat the Rudra, interrupting the enraged little man.

"Take him away," ordered the warden, with a growl.

Mr White wrapped an enormous hand, around the Rudra's arm, it felt painful to touch him, as if acid had spilled on the man, forcing the cyborg to let go with a jolt.

"Thank you," said the naked inmate, sarcastically.

"When you see Rico, do tell him to pop over for a chat, will you? I have something of his," he continued, addressing the agents as he was led away, by White and his squad, planting the seed for later.

"Will do," said Malone politely.

"On it sir," whispered agent Jeffries, Malone nodded in approval.

"Time for us turn in, enjoy the rest of your afternoon now, ya hear," said special agent sterling, backing towards an open panel with Jeffries and Malone. weapons drawn and ready.

"Good to see you, in chains again," said Malone.

"At least we know where to find you," added special agent Jeffries, to the Rudra.

"Indeed," answered the Rudra, smiling slightly as the squad of armed men, led by the cyborg Mr White, nudged him along.

"Take Him to the hole," ordered the warden, as the large group of men, set off with the naked man.

"And for God's sake, get some rags on that convict before it gets any colder," continued the warden, trying to mock the Rudra as he was escorted bodily, out of the door at gunpoint.

"And as for you Malone," began the furious warden, turning towards the special agents. His eyes opened wide in panic, they had vanished out of the secret exits, using the warden's own trick against him.

"SHIT, SHIT, Shitty, Shit, shit," shouted the warden, losing his temper and slamming his fist, into the large wooden desk.

He looked around the empty room, got up wearily and closed the thick door with a slam. The vile creature waddled over to the viewing window and drew the blinds with a sigh.

The warden collapsed into his rhino leather chair, reached into his, lower desk drawer and poured himself, a large crystal tumbler, of single malt.

The animal necked it, like it was water. The expensive liquid dripped from his greedy mouth and ran down his face and neck, adding one more stain, to his filthy, tattered, white linen shirt.

The elaborate, abstract ceiling mural began slowly and subtly moving above him.

"Shit," said the warden, his voice choked to a whisper.

The warden drained the last drop of whisky and hurriedly, wiped his face in a feeble attempt at smartening himself up.

The fretful warden pushed himself, up against the back support, of the large chair and snatched the grubby white Panama from his sweat drenched, head. He looked up towards the moving mural for guidance and order, but to his astonishment, the shapes and lines had become still.

"Son, we need to talk," came a cold gruff voice, from in front of the foul man. The warden snapped his head towards the origin, of that voice in Terror.

San Diablo, the devils haven.

CHAPTER 25.

The warden opened his eyes, to an empty room, he could sense though, the presence of, the Lord of evil.

The trembling sack of filth, lent over his large wooden desk and peered over the far edge of the ornate trim. He stared at the floor in disbelief and horror.

Two large, red horns, began slowly rising up from the warden's office floor. A large, terrifying head and face rose up, joining the long-curved horns, in the office.

Slowly, but not slowly enough for the warden, a broad, demonic looking man, in a sharp and exquisitely tailored suit, appeared in the space in front of the trembling, warden's desk, rising up from the ground.

The formidable sight, of the risen Lord of evil, limped towards the small, round man and with a hop, sat on the large wooden desk.

The warden tried desperately, to move away from the sitting demon king, but to his horror, found he could not move a muscle. He was paralysed, by the demon's, dark power. An unwilling captive, frozen like a statue by the will of his master, the risen Lucifer himself.

"I'm disappointed son, really, REALLY, disappointed," said the devil, in a deep and frightening voice.

El diablo raised a finger in the air and the warden, wincing in pain, rose out of his chair involuntary, and by the power of the dark Lords will, flew out of the chair and slammed into the window behind him, as if grabbed by the throat, by an invisible assailant.

"Get rid of Malone and his men," ordered the menacing King of Hell.

"H, h, h how?" asked the warden, his words trapped in his crushed wind pipe.

"Take them to the Doc," snarled the demon, walking towards the throttled man. The warden rose up off his feet, until he was face to face, with the tall, demon king.

"Yes, yes, my master," simpered the warden, pathetic in fear.

The frightened warden, thought it best not to mention the Aghori on route to the hole, but instead chose to stay silent on the matter.

The terrifying demon king, gently wrapped his long thick fingers, around the trapped wardens left arm, lifting it up to face height.

"You don't mind, do you?" he said, licking his sharp teeth, with a red, forked tongue.

"I'm fucking ravenous," roared the beast, tipping his head back in sadistic laughter.

With a disgusting crunch, El Diablo bit off the wardens left hand, chewing it slowly and deliberately in front of the screaming man.

He chewed sadistically for a while and swallowed the appendage, belching in the man's face.

"Do not fail me again! Ready the slaves for our arrival...
No more fuck ups, understand?" Demanded the demon
king, menacingly.

The warden was silent, caught up in pain and fear.

Lucifer threw the fat man, across the room in rage.

"I said, fucking understand!!" bellowed the frightening
monstrosity.

The warden nodded his head frantically.

"Yes, my Lord, all shall be prepared, for your glorious
return," said the warden, picking himself up from the
floor.

"It had better," growled the demon, vanishing into thin
air, like a wisp of smoke.

The livid warden made his way, back to his chair and
slumped heavily at his desk. Watching his stubby hand
grow, slowly and painfully back.

He winced in pain, as he wriggled his fingers. The skin
grew back over his red, raw, fleshy hand and wrist. He
took a deep breath in, as the agony, of fingernails re-

growing through exposed and raw fingertips, filled his world.

Mr Whites radio Comms, suddenly barked into life with the anguished voice of the warden, barking over the speaker.

White, drop that sack of shit at the hole and get your steroid, black ass, back up here, and bring the ghosts," spat the disgusting man, with a scream.

"As you command," replied Mr White, blankly to his shoulder Comms.

Mr White and his squad, advanced steadily through the segregation unit and into the yard, via a maze of razor wire covered, electronic fence partitions and checkpoints. They eventually entered the segregation, punishment and behaviour modification facility.

The hole.

The party arrived at a small wooden cube, around four feet each way, with a small opening on the front, big enough to fit a food tray through.

They stopped and fanned around the Aghori at gunpoint. Twenty plus gun barrels, pressed hard into the Rudra's neck and body.

The Rudra began to twitch and jerk, then fold himself over for a few moments, before standing up and handing a broken pair of titanium hand cuffs, to Mr White.

The armed men, hesitant with shock, looked at each other uneasily, for a sign of what to do next. As Mr White silently took the broken restraints, from the naked Aghori, his eyes never moved from him.

The big cyborg held a hand up, to gain the attention of his squad, a gesture that said hold your position, but be ready to open fire.

"Don't let me keep you chaps, I'll see myself in," said the Rudra, genially, while opening the front panel, of the tiny, rabbit hutch of a cell.

He bent forward and entered into the dark, claustrophobic space.

The door slammed behind him, totally extinguishing the light.

The outside world was shut out, all but the sliding, clicking noise, of bars and locks banging into position.

"Ahh, home sweet home," said the Rudra cheerfully to the guards, as he settled in for a busy night ahead.

Epilogue.

Pappa Smurf took a large, final drag on his cigarette, enjoying the intrigue he had unleashed into the interview room. He paused for a moment, lungs full of acrid smoke and gazed over the room full of journalist and office staff, all absent from their tasks, hanging instead, on the warrior monks every word.

He blew a thick plume of smoke into the room, masking the gaggle of spellbound reporters, in a fog of second-hand smoke.

One of the reporters, a man in his thirties with thick blond hair, began coughing and began to stand, as if to protest.

Pappa Smurf locked his gaze on the man, with a growl, cowing the paparazzi to silence.

The inmate monk extinguished his cigarette, into the palm of his hand. The muscular monk smiled as the hot ember, burned into his flesh.

"Why don't you just escape, I mean, you're the one that hunts, why don't you escape and have a normal life?" asked Sharon, one of Gitas older colleagues. She was transfixed on the man totally.

"Escape? Oh, my dear, you're missing the flow playa, that's why I do this, to escape the Hell that awaits me." Pappa Smurf stared blankly into the middle space of the room for a moment, lost in his own world of thought and memory.

"I've seen what awaits men like me and I know, that to avoid that fate, I must make right what I have done, weather I avoid Hell or not, I must serve my masters will, with everything that I have." continued the ex-gang leader, Pappa Smurf.

"What about the CIA men? Did they escape?" asked Gita, voice recorder in hand, hungry for the rest of his story.

"Oh of course not, agents like that do not escape baby, they serve," answered Pappa Smurf, through a chuckle.

"And the Rudra?" asked the coughing man, finding his voice again and his courage.

"What about him?" snapped the bad ass inmate monk.

"Did the warden teach him some manners, once the Rudra became his prisoner?" continued the man, rightly trembling in the monks, dominating presence.

"The Rudra? A prisoner? No how would you imprison the sun light, is it possible? No of course not, you cannot find a cage big enough, to hold the universe captive and you cannot put handcuffs on God, but the evil warden himself, in his arrogance thought he would be the one to do it," said Pappa Smurf, the fire of wrath in his eye.

A loud knock at the interview room door, made all in the room jump, all except the mysterious fighting monk, from San Diablo.

"Come!" ordered Pappa Smurf, to the maker of the knock.

A thick set, muscular man, in his late thirties entered the room. The man, also a black robed monk, bent at the knees and lay prostrate on the ground, he was absolutely covered in tattoos, Nazi insignia and symbols of gang loyalties, etched into the vicious looking Caucasian man's skin.

Pappa Smurf clapped his huge hands together once, freeing the lowrider monk from protocol.

"What is it brother Shooter?" boomed the huge, African American superior.

Shooter jumped to his feet and bowed in respect.

"He has come brother and demands your presence." said the younger monk, while bent slightly, bowing to the great man.

Without saying a word, the elder monk rose from his chair.

"Who is waiting for you?" asked Gita, hurriedly to the back of the two men, leaving the room.

"The supreme person, Shri Rudra," answered the monk, walking out of the interview room door.

"But our interview, erm, erm, venerable Sir?" shouted the ambitious journalist, to the closing door and the enigmatic warrior monk, Pappa Smurf.

"To be continued bitch," roared the elder monk, with a deep, but fading laugh.

"They had all heard the rumours of the place of course, but they had dismissed them as rumour and BS. The prison doctor would pronounce you dead,,,

And you would disappear from heart and memory and enter into Hell.

San Diablo, the devils haven, is set in the middle of the baking hot Nevada desert, hidden from public view and scrutiny. A super top scret, super max facility for the very worst of the worst, those dead to society and the world, those who no one would miss.

It soon becomes clear that all is not how it seems at San Diablo,miether is the sadistic warden, or the bizzar new inmate, the latest guest of the wardens devils haven,or even the C,I,A agents themselves,axactly what they seem.

Printed in Great Britain
by Amazon